A Garland Series
Foundations of the Novel

Representative Early

Eighteenth-Century Fiction

A collection of 100 rare titles
reprinted in photo-facsimile in 71 volumes

Foundations of the Novel

compiled and edited by
Michael F. Shugrue
Secretary for English for the M.L.A.

with New Introductions for each volume by

Michael Shugrue, *City College of C.U.N.Y.*
Malcolm J. Bosse, *City College of C.U.N.Y.*
William Graves, *N.Y. Institute of Technology*
Josephine Grieder, *Rutgers University, Newark*

The Court and City Vagaries
Anonymous

The Tell-Tale
Anonymous

Entertainments of Gallantry
Anonymous

with a new introduction
for the Garland Edition by
Josephine Grieder

Garland Publishing, Inc., New York & London

1973

The new introduction for the

Garland *Foundations of the Novel* Edition

is Copyright © 1973, by

Garland *Publishing, Inc., New York & London*

All Rights Reserved

Library of Congress Cataloging in Publication Data
Main entry under title:

The Court and city vagaries.

    (Foundations of the novel)
    Facsim. reprint of three works. Original t. p. of
the 1st work published 1711? reads: The court and city
vagaries, or intrigues of both sexes. Written by one of
the fair sex. London, Printed and sold by J. Baker ...
Original t.p. of the 2d reads: The tell-tale; or the
invisible witness: being the secret observations of
Philologus upon the private actions of human life. ...
London, Printed for A. Baldwin...1711. Original t.p.
of the 3d reads: Entertainments of gallantry, or
remedies for love. Familiarly discours'd by a society
of persons of quality ... London, Printed for John
Morphew ... 1712.
    1. English fiction--18th century. I. Philologus,
pseud. The tell-take. 1973. II. Entertainments of
gallantry. 1973. III. Series.
PZ1.C843 1711a [PR1297]   823'.03   70-170525
ISBN 8240-0530-9

Printed in the United States of America

Introduction

The emergence of the novel as a bona fide literary genre during the eighteenth century is, to be sure, best studied in the works of masters like Fielding and Richardson. But since the novel, unlike the goddess, did not spring full-grown from the forehead of its creators, the study of humbler efforts has its place in literary history, for in these minor works can be traced the tentative gropings toward technique and structure that more talented authors would later perfect. Of particular interest in this respect is the fiction of the first two decades of the century, for, as Lionel Stevenson says, "The separate ingredients for realistic novels were developing in miscellaneous forms."[1] *The volumes here reprinted* – The Court and City Vagaries, The Tell-Tale, *and* Entertainments of Gallantry – *bear out his observation.*

The Court and City Vagaries; or Intrigues, of Both Sexes *is the authoress' first-person narrative of anecdotes about her and her acquaintances. One of Stevenson's ingredients, the Theophrastian portrait, finds its way into her recital in the description of Lady Tuneal. A widow and a man hater, she devotes herself to the piano; and her conversation, reported directly, proves her as sententious and vague as the authoress alleges her to be. But the work's principal interest lies in the*

INTRODUCTION

various anecdotes which, as in real life, happen more or less coincidentally to ordinary people and which have neither a particular climax nor a point to make. In the first anecdote, for example, two strictly raised young ladies from the city sneak off to St. James's Park, where they try to pass themselves off as aristocracy. Their ruse succeeds only in attracting a young rake, who, more experienced than they, gets them to a Haymarket tavern and beats them till they pawn their jewels and buy their liberty. In another, Lady Sparkit, who has been loved and left by her unfaithful husband, accidentally mistakes another man for her spouse and, in her desire to retrieve his conjugal affection, finds herself involved with the amorous Lord Newlove. The authoress is not above laughing at herself, either, as she relates an adventure with her neighbor; interpreting his behavior as excessively lover-like, she prepares in advance a letter advising him to be more prudent — only to receive from him a letter giving her precisely the same advice. The tone of the anecdotes is playful and the details and settings unprepossessing but realistic.

Entertainments of Gallantry; or Remedies for Love *represents another of Stevenson's ingredients for fiction, the imaginary dialogue in the tradition of Lucian and Erasmus. Nor is it without echoes of Boccaccio, as a select society of ladies and gentlemen assembled at Epsom to take the waters decides to amuse itself with six days of conversation and stories. The bulk of the work consists of their direct commentaries on passages from Ovid's* Remedium [sic] Amoris, *but they enliven*

INTRODUCTION

their opinions with stories illustrating such eternal topics as woman's fickleness, jealousy, and maidenly modesty. Little pretense is made by the author at realistic detail or characterization — only one person even has a name — but their observations on love will turn up as amorous commonplaces in later fiction. "Love is the only Passion of the Heart," remarks one; "There is nothing can come in Competition with it, much less eradicate it" (p. 17). "These first Amours are always most violent," observes another; "Time can hardly extinguish 'em; Death alone totally eradicate 'em; and a Heart thus prepossess'd, retains with vast Delight, the Object of his first Desires" (p. 32).

The Tell-Tale; or the Invisible Witness *has perhaps the best claim of the three to fictional structure, for in spite of his digressions, Philologus narrates reasonably directly the affairs of his faithless mistress Millamant with Colonel Sinecure,* "her fifteenth Coxcomb in waiting" (p. 12), *and Robin Rough, the lord she eventually marries. The author is, however, indebted to Le Sage and* Le Diable Boiteux *for his basic mechanism: for Philologus is allowed these glimpses of his beloved as the invisible guest of Philadel, a grateful young spirit whom he liberated by accident from captivity in an oak.*[2]

The tone of The Tell-Tale *resembles that of* Court and City Vagaries, *light, playful, and indulgently mocking. Philologus becomes annoyed with the literary criticism of a young man who had* "taken his Wits Degree at Will's Coffee-House" (p. 15); *he writes to the faithless Millamant,* "the Weather is as warm as your

INTRODUCTION

Youth; and you may now venture to leave off a Lover like your Tippet, without catching Cold or Scandal" (p. 9); he reports with amusement Robin Rough's multiple attempts to compose a subtle letter of reproach to the coquette. Even the end of the novel has a nicely ironic twist: after their marriage, Robin Rough declares to Millamant that he has married her only out of spite and vows *"to sacrifice the future Quiet of my Life to make yours effectually miserable"* (p. 62); she retaliates by confessing her glee at having reduced him to such a state and promising to exacerbate his feelings further; *"and both putting on a well-bred Smile of Contempt, they retir'd to their separate Apartments"* (p. 65).

All three of these works are anonymous; none achieved a second edition; and though the authors of The Tell-Tale *and* Court *and* City Vagaries *promise continuations, they never kept their word. These facts, seemingly unrelated, do at least point to the amateur standing, if so it may be called, of prose fiction during the period. In a genre lacking as yet form or rules, any amateur may try his hand. If his work is not cherished by posterity, it exists at least as testimony to the interests and experimentation that more masterful writers were soon to capitalize upon.*

Josephine Grieder

INTRODUCTION

NOTES

[1] The English Novel, a Panorama *(Boston: Houghton Mifflin Co., 1960), p. 55.*

[2] *Hints of Scarron and his* roman comique *also surface in Philologus' deliberate vagueness as to precise details of time and names and his frequent asides to the reader.*

The Court and City Vagaries

Anonymous

Bibliographical note:
This facsimile has been made from a copy in the Houghton Library of Harvard University (*EC7 A100 711c7)

THE
Court and City
Vagaries,
OR
Intrigues,
OF
Both Sexes.

Written by one of the fair Sex.

LONDON,

Printed: And Sold by *J. Baker*, at the *Black Boy* in *Pater-Noster-Row*.

Price Six-Pence.

TO THE
AUTHOR.

AT last, my dear Idalia, *I have detected the fair Criminal, and found out your little wanton Frauds, in concealing a legitimate Birth of your Brain from me : But, upon second Thoughts, I am satisfy'd your Modesty has deny'd me the Priviledge of assisting your Labour, and congratulating you upon so hopeful an Issue. Had I suspected you so near your Time, I should have attended the first Cry, and look'd upon the Offspring with all the forward and officious Sentiments of a Friend. You could have no ways defended your self from a Partiality to your Cause, but by maintaining a Privacy. Methinks I trac'd you in every Feature ; each beauteous Lineament confessed the happy Mother ; but still I was at a Loss. The kindly Stamp betray'd the innocent Original ; and I was often feeling the*
Goddess

The PREFACE.

Goddess thro' the thin Drapery. You are so happy, my charming Idalia, *in your native Charms, that you will never covet borrow'd Ornaments.*

There's no altering your Charms; the least Manly Stroke, as it would take from the Softness of the She-Pencil, so it would add a disagreeable Varnish to the tender Colours you have laid on. The sole Fault I find in you, is, that you have moraliz'd at an Age of innocent Liberties. It crosses upon Nature, to see a young Philosopher in Petticoats giving Cautions against Experiments, that every young Lady should be in some Measure acquainted with, to guard her against future Insults. Such Adventures as you represent in your first Scene, might be acted to Improvement, had not a dishonourable Bully been the first Aggressor. The only Way to know the Artifices of perfidious Man, is to converse with them at large; and the affected Vows and Tenderness of that Sex, should be decently known, before the regular Attacks in an honourable Way for Life. Go on, my fair Maid, in Pursuit of these amorous Mistakes; lash the barbarous Part of our Sex, but indulge to the harmless Tenders of a well-natur'd Swain, and make Damon *and* Pastora *happy from Twenty to Thirty.*

THE
Court and City Figaries
OF
BOTH SEXES.

I SHALL begin with a remarkable Paſſage that happen'd very lately; which I hope may ſerve by Way of Caution to all young Ladies, who are induſtriouſly ſearching out the Knowledge of Ill, with a pious Deſign to avoid it.

Aminda and *Ciladira*, two very handſome, well-bred, religious, young Women, of the firſt Rank in the City; I'll aſſure you, Ladies of the niceſt Reputation, which may be obſerv'd in their grave Looks and ſedate Behaviours, and I believe may juſtly deſerve the Character of Women of Honour. They are kept under great Reſtraints by their Parents; which, with a natural Deſire

Defire of adding new Conquefts to a Crowd of Admirers, has put them upon an Humour of regaling themfelves in private, and, as often as Opportunity ferves, to go in Search of Adventures, by Way of Amufement; which Diverfions they have follow'd for fome Time, with great Succefs, both at Home and Abroad, and never fail to return victorious. This has encourag'd 'em to proceed with greater Refolution than ever, being obftinately opinionated of their own Conduct.

These Ladies are pretty often feen at *Hide-Park*, under the Cuftody of *Ciladira*'s Mother; but one Day having got the Coach to themfelves, the Weather being extream pleafant, were, refolv'd not to lofe Time and Opportunity, but gave Orders forthwith to be fet down at a Relation's in *Weftminfter*; where, after a fhort Vifit, they difmifs'd the Coach, with a Meffage, that they were oblig'd to ftay there at Supper, and fhould take a Hack to come Home. They had another Excufe as ready to the Lady of the Houfe, for taking Leave in fuch Hafte; and accordingly make the beft of their Way for St. *James's-Park*, where they had not been long, before they had the Pleafure to find their Beauty attract all Eyes; and no Doubt but they heard a great many Sighs and Whifpers, as they

they mov'd thro' the gazing Crowd of Beaux that flutter'd around 'em: All which pass'd for good Omens, tho' as yet none durst assume the Courage to attack 'em. At last, one more daring than the rest, draws near, keeps Pace, curiously surveys and attends their Motions. They took the Hint, views him as strictly, and by his Garb, Air, and Deportment, easily perceiv'd him, as they imagin'd, to be of Quality. He had not waited long for an Opportunity to introduce his Discourse, before one offers it self; which was, to resolve something they were disputing on. The Ladies being bent on a Frolick, if they lik'd the Person that should make an Attempt, were not very hard of Access, and especially to so fine a Gentleman as this, endeavour'd to make themselves as pleasing and agreeable as possible. The Hero is so absolutely charm'd with their Appearance and Conversation, that he believes himself no longer on Earth; *Or rather*, said he, *these are real Goddesses, descended from their Celestial Habitations, not only to dazzle the Eyes, and inflame the Hearts, but to punish all with Death, who have the daring Impudence to approach 'em.* And being now darkish, claps down on his Knees, closes his Hands, and implores Pardon for his sacrilegious Attempt. The Girls,

Girls, seeing themselves thus idoliz'd, began to think there was something in it. Immediately one fancies she is *Diana*, and the other *Pallas*; but upon farther Reflexion, found they had Reason to confess themselves meer Mortals, and subject to Human Frailties; as indeed it prov'd in the Conclusion. *Damon* was very difficultly brought to believe they were so: But however, finding his Company did not displease, ventures from one Degree to another, to come to a better Understanding with them. He knew the World throughly, or at least the baser Part; and easily judg'd who he had to deal with. Their Innocence and Rank, were visible in their Persons and Behaviours; so that he needs not make much Search into that, but took Opportunity, on all Occasions, to let them understand his Quality, as in this Manner; *We were a great many Noblemen at Dinner with the Duke of* ——— *to Day*; and when any Body answer'd him, it was, *My Lord*, says he, *or your Lordship may command me on all Occasions*, and so on, with a great many very entertaining Stories. After some Time spent thus agreeably, the Ladies were oblig'd to think of returning Home. *Damon* eagerly presses for the Honour to hand em into their Coach. They answer'd, that was already dismiss'd, and should

should therefore spare him that unnecessary Trouble. He then offers 'em his Chariot and Equipage that waited; and to compleat the Victory, he declar'd *Aminda* had gain'd over his Heart, and that he himself would attend at her Chariot Wheels. This great Complement and Condescention, in a Person of this Distinction, serv'd to encrease that good Opinion and Esteem she had already receiv'd of him. However, this Offer could not be accepted, for several Reasons, which he suffer'd himself to be convinc'd of; but still persisted in his Design of conducting them safe Home, and pretended he must step on one Side, and leave Orders with his Servants where to wait on him afterwards. He was no sooner gone, but *Aminda* began to extol his Person and extraordinary Qualifications, to the highest Degree imaginable, and said she found so much Difference between the Conversation of a Man of Quality, and that of a private Gentleman, that indeed she believ'd she should hardly prevail with herself hereafter, to make the latter a tolerable civil Answer, if he should ever attempt to make Love to her. Whether *Ciladira* had really a truer Taste, or whether it was Envy to her Companion, because he address'd himself more particularly to her, said she could not believe him what he would appear

pear to be; and would have continu'd on that Subject, but *Aminda* would by no Means encourage such dishonourable Apprehensions. By this Time *Damon* was return'd, and made what Haste he could to usher 'em into a Hackney-Coach he had provided, where they were no sooner enter'd, but he began to entreat they would permit him to treat 'em with some Jellies, and Ice-Creams, at *White*'s Chocolate-house, The Windows being drawn up, it was impossible to discover them. These, with a great many other Perswasions, prevail'd, and the Ladies grow easy, and extreamly delighted; upon which, the Spark takes Advantage to recommend innocent Diversions above all Things, and rails at all impertinent old Women; who, because they are past the Enjoyments of Life, are envious of those who ought to possess 'em, and render Pleasures as dangerous and pernicious, with frightful *Ideas*, devis'd to keep Fools in Ignorance, and so consequently under their Jurisdiction; but that so much Beauty, with all the Perfection Nature could bestow, was not given 'em with Design to be bury'd in Oblivion: And to depart out of the World, just as they came into it, would prove to little Purpose. Those strong Arguments overcame all the weak ones they could bring in Opposition, and

at

at laſt were oblig'd to yield the Debate, reſign to his Diſcretion for that Time, and ſuffer themſelves to be convey'd to a Tavern in the *Hay-Market*. I beg the Ladies Pardon, for ſpeaking ſo very plain; but however, if they can keep their own Countenance, and refrain from bluſhing, it ſhall never go farther for me. After a ſplended Entertainment, and abundance of Compliments paſs'd on all Sides, it grew late, and the Ladies were very uneaſy to be going Home. He ſaid it was too early yet, deſires 'em to take off their Glaſſes with Chearfulneſs, and be thankful. This Speech gave them the firſt Allarm; but they did not know whether to take it as Jeſt or Earneſt. He goes on, and bids 'em conſider between themſelves, whether they would both or one go Home with him to his Lodgings. Upon this, they aſk'd, with a great deal of Indignation, which ſufficiently expreſs'd their Surprize and Reſentment, what he meant, and who he took them for. He anſwers: *Look ye, Ladies, ye may put on Diſguiſe, and give your ſelves what Airs you pleaſe; but at this Time ye have miſs'd your Aim. I know the World too well to be impos'd on.* You'll gueſs, by this Time, *Aminda* began to repent her Choice of a Lover, and *Ciladira* as much enrag'd to have her Judgment neglected,

lected, gave her Friend a severe Reprimand for drawing her into the Snare, contrary to her own Inclinations, which perhaps their utmost Care and Politicks could not disentangle. *Aminda* falls upon him with high Words, in Hopes to over-power him that Way; but finding this Stratagem fail, she was oblig'd to alter the Scheme, and endeavour to sooth him into good Nature. At last, with abundance of Difficulty, they manag'd it so as to quit the House, but could not possibly get quit of the Rascal. He was resolv'd to pursue 'em to Destruction, lays violent Hands on *Aminda*, dragging her towards the *Strand*, pinching and tormenting her in a grievous Manner. *Ciladira* pursu'd as fast as she could, and both join'd their Prayers and Entreaties in vain to this inflexible Barbarian; for all the Return they could get, was, That when he met with such Jilts, he knew how to use 'em: That they had urg'd him to spend a great deal of Money, he could employ much better; and swore he would have Satisfaction one Way or other, before they parted; and would therefore give 'em three Things to chuse, *viz.* Go and lie with him all Night, or be secur'd in the *Round-house*, or else return all the Money he had deposited on their Accounts. *Ciladira* was glad to find they might have their Liberty on
this

this laſt Condition, and deſir'd to know how much they were indebted to him; he anſwer'd, Five Guineas. She was then at as great a Loſs as ever, knowing at that Time they had ſcarce one between 'em; but ſaid, if he would let them know where to direct, ſhe would give her Word and Honour it ſhould be ſent him next Day without fail. As this Scoundrel had no Notion of Honour, ſo it prov'd to as little Purpoſe to make him ſuch Propoſitions. He ſaw 'em well dreſs'd, and adorn'd with Jewels of conſiderable Value, eſpecially *Aminda*, whom he made his particular Ward; and, like a true Infernal, never ceas'd to torture and afflict, beſides tearing her fine lac'd Lappits and Ruffles all to Rags. He obſerv'd *Ciladira* had only a Gold Watch and Diamond Ring, which he bid her leave in his Cuſtody, 'till ſhe could perform her Promiſe; but not being willing to do this, he order'd her to pawn 'em at a Tavern in St. *Martins-Lane*, where he had dragg'd them with Deſign for that *Round-houſe*, if other Projects fail'd. By this Time the Watch had Notice, and were haſtening to ſecure them all; which *Ciladira* prevented, by declaring their Innocence and Diſaſter in ſo moving a Manner, together with a little Money to drink her Health, that ſhe prevail'd upon them to

C withdraw,

withdraw. She runs in this Confusion, and procur'd the Money, deliver'd it to him immediately, and demands her Companion, who stood trembling, lamenting, and almost dying in the Hands of her Persecutor. He tells her they had not adjusted all Matters yet; but for her own Part, since she had defray'd the Expences he had been at, he was content to permit her the Freedom of going Home when she pleas'd; but for this little saucy Jilt, he had another Reckoning to make with her, both for her Insolence, and his Loss of Time, which she must account for before they part. This last Demand struck them into the greatest Horror and Despair imaginable, while he redoubled his Oaths to make her a publick Example. *Ciladira*, who has a Soul truly brave and compassionate, disdaining the mean Considerations of Self-Preservation, chose rather to undergo those present Inconveniencies, together with the Hazard of future Advantages, than to abandon her Friend in Distress, desir'd to know how she must redeem her from Bondage. Bully answer'd, the Thing depended on herself, that Diamond Cross which hangs, as a needless Addition, on her more illustrious Bosom, will pawn for ten Guineas, to purchase her Liberty. *Aminda* was cut to the Heart, with the Apprehension of losing her

her belov'd Ornaments, to which she is so extreamly bigotted, that she would endanger her eternal Reputation, and suffer all the Punishment he could inflict, rather than part with any one of them. *Ciladira* knowing her Temper and Resolution, went and engag'd her Watch, as she had before her Ring, and was returning, when a Gentleman seiz'd her in his Arms, calling her Angel and Goddess, with a great many such Speeches. She was ready to swoon at the Repetition of what had betray'd her to this; but seeing some promising Appearances in him, she cast herself at his Feet, and begg'd he would pity a distressed Maid. He was extreamly mov'd with her Request; and looking upon her with a more different Regard than those who are accustom'd to such Disorders, generously offer'd his Assistance against all Insults or Affronts that might be offer'd her, and that he was resolv'd to protect and defend her with the last Drop of his Blood. This Cavalier is a Colonel in the Army, has a great deal of Honour, and real Courage, which he had signaliz'd on several Occasions. *Ciladira* was much comforted to meet with a Knight-Errant; but however, to prevent a Quarrel, least it might prove a Means to expose 'em, clapt the Guineas into his Hand, catch'd Hold of *Aminda*, return'd him many Thanks, and fo would have parted. No Doubt the Sharper was well fatisfy'd with this, efpecially when he faw a Gentleman who faid he was a near Relation, and fufpecting fomething more than ordinary, took Hold of his Hand, and defir'd to know for what Reafon he had receiv'd that Money; would have urg'd him in to drink a Bottle of Wine, and inform him how far he was oblig'd to him on the Account of thofe Ladies. The poor Fellow, who durft not contend with any but thofe who could not defend themfelves, turn'd pale as Death, fhrunk back, and only faid the Ladies were very welcome, bow'd, and wifh'd it had been in his Power to have ferv'd them farther. *Ciladira* was glad to let this pafs, leaft he fhould difcover any Thing to their Difadvantage, and faid, that the Obligations they had to this Gentleman, were for freeing 'em from the Clamour of a Hackney Coach-man, who had impos'd a great deal more than his Due, and not having Money enough about 'em, he had been fo kind to lend 'em a Crown, which was what he faw her return him. This pafs'd pretty well on all Sides, and the Spark made off as faft as he could, throughly glad of this Night's Succefs. The Colonel begg'd to 'fquire them Home, and did not fail to make abundance of Complements by the

Way,

Way, for the Honour they had done, in admitting him rather than the other: But having cast his Eyes on *Aminda*, and observing her Cloths so disorder'd, and her Looks so sorrowful, imagin'd she had had foul Play, and with Difficulty brought 'em to confess their ill Usage, tho' they carefully omitted that Part of the Story that reflects on their Conduct. He chid 'em severely for not putting it in his Power to retrieve their Losses, and chastise the Villain. At parting, he extreamly importun'd *Ciladira* to honour him with a Line or two, directed to *Man's* Coffee-house; which she promis'd to do, as a grateful Acknowledgment for the Service he had done them; and I suppose went to Bed sufficiently mortify'd with their Adventure.

AMongst all my Acquaintance, I never observ'd any so compleatly whimsical, and remarkable of herself, (and is that they call something so entirely out of the Way) as Lady *Tuneal*. She is a Woman of Quality, a great Pretender to Vertue, Wit, and Discretion, with a Mixture of Philosophical Notions, and may with Justice stile herself—a Person—every Way distininguishable; and tho' she be a professs'd fels'd Man-hater, yet has neverthelefs, thro' the Sollicitations of her Friends, been prevail'd with to enter into a conjugal State, much to her own Diffatisfaction; but had the good Fortune, after fome few Years, to be releas'd from him to whom fhe caufelefsly bore fo much Averfion, and plac'd as the Center of all her Uneafinefs and Difquiets. She is fo far from playing the Hypocrite on this Account, that fhe openly declares a Diflike and ill Opinion of all Women, who do not agree with her Sentiments on the fame Occafion, and can never believe, but that a Woman of Vertue will always efteem it her greateft Blefling to be freed from thofe filthy—ufelefs—lumbering—Male-Creatures. She has one only Daughter, Heirefs to a plentiful Fortune, and every Way deferving; but I think her Ladyfhip does not feem to place much Joy in her, or indeed any Thing this Earth produces, excepting her moft dearly beloved Spinet; to which fhe is fo entirely devoted, that fhe thinks every Moment loft, that is not employ'd in the Improvement of this out-of-Fafhion Inftrument of Mufick. She not only makes it the Bufinefs of her Life, but, as tho' her future Happinefs depended thereon, fuffers nothing to intercept; but if fhe be oblig'd fometimes, tho' with great Regret,

to

to receive what she calls impertinent Visits, she is forc'd to sit up very late, nay, often the whole Night, before she can make a Repetition of all her Tunes; which she never fails to do, before she sleeps. She has a singular Method in every Thing she says and does, and is attended with an Imperfection, I suppose rather habitual, than natural; which generally proves the greatest Hinderance to her Employment or Diversion; that is, she can never speak of the least Thing, or give any necessary Orders in her Family, without Multiplicity of useless Words, and will fetch every Thing so very far about, that it's impossible to guess what she aims to conclude in. Every one of those Words must be distinctly utter'd, with a Pause which lasts a Minute, or more, according as she requires Time to sigh and breathe in; so that one has lost the Beginning of the Sentence, before one can learn the latter End. It's not long since a Lady call'd on me, to wait on Lady *Tuneal*. We found her at her usual Pass-time, but in pleasanter Temper than ordinary. She no sooner observ'd us in a Posture of going, but she began to intreat our Stay, declar'd she was never better pleas'd in Company, and that she did really esteem us as Persons of Discretion; and therefore hop'd we should dispence with her, as to those Formalities and
Deco-

Decorums, which might not anſwer at this Time with her Conveniency; for having been that Day much interrupted in her Muſick, ſhould therefore be oblig'd to ſit up late, which always proves extreamly prejudicial to her Health. We beg'd her Ladyſhip to uſe us with the ſame Familiarity ſhe would her Daughter, or thoſe of her Attendance. After we had been agreeably enough entertain'd for ſome Time, with ſeveral new Tunes, of which ſhe is never unprovided, at the ſet Time, according to her Cuſtom, which is as unalterable as the Laws of the *Medes* and *Perſians*, ſhe rings her Bell; upon which, Mrs. *Smart*, her Woman, deſires to know her Ladyſhip's Pleaſure. She begins, Smart,— *I have call'd you with Intention—to conſult—about Supper.*— Her Woman propos'd ſeveral Things, which I thought proper for Night; but my Lady looks frighted, turns pail, and proteſts ſhe has given her the Spleen to the higheſt Degree, in naming ſuch groſs Meats at this unſeaſonable Hour, and at laſt recovers Breath to cry out,— Smart,— *you are a Perſon—of a hail Conſtitution;— but when a Perſon—has liv'd ſo long with—a Perſon of Quality,— there might be gathering up—ſome Fragments of Senſe,—at leaſt enough to—diſtinguiſh them— from the Commonalty: — But—to ſpeak yet plainer*

plainer still,— tho' with abundance —of Difficulty,— for want of Breath,— as well as Loss of Time,— which to me—is always precious,— very precious,— tho' not so with you,— and the unthinking World;— yet, I do say,— you might have distinguish'd mine —from vulgar Appetites;— have spar'd me all these Considerations,— and have come with—something ready projected,— suitable to the—Delicacy of my Palate,—and Tenderness—of Constitution withal,— by way of Cordial,— to revive decaying Spirits.—

Smart answer'd her Lady, that she had nam'd what she knew of, to be proper in all those Cases; and that she dare say, if the Truth were known, her Ladyship had herself projected the Supper she design'd, and only urg'd all this to try if she could divine; which in all Likelihood might prove as difficult, as it was for the *South*-Sayers and Magicians to tell King *Nebuchadnezzar* not only the Interpretation, but the Dream too: But if she would let her have her Commands in a Word, she should readily be obey'd. The Lady reply'd, *Why, truly,* Smart,*— I have observ'd you to be —a Person—always ready furnish'd—with a Stock of Spirits,— and so consequently always on a Hurry;— and since you will reduce me—to the Necessity—of naming the Thing—my self, I desire you'll step down—*

D into

into the Kitchen, and leave Orders—with the Cook—to make me—half a Porringer—of Water-Gruel.— Smart, not a little glad to receive the Message, in Hopes to be dismiss'd for that Time, was going in all Haste to deliver it, when her Lady calls her back, with a Charge to let it be thin, very thin. She was no sooner dispatch'd with these second Orders, but was again recalled to take a more strict one yet, which was, that it must not exceed half a Porringer, but rather abate something of half a Porringer, and to be sure that it be Poverty-Gruel. After this, she falls to shaking her Fingers on the Spinet, with greater Vehemency than ever; which put her into such Disorder, that she was oblig'd to desist, and recover Strength, by sighing and gasping afresh. *Smart* finding her Lady in such Extremities, propos'd to have a Spoon-full of Sack in the Gruel, as a comfortable Cordial, and might incline her to Rest: Upon which, she sinks into her Chair, struggles for new Life, and profess'd that she was absolutely overcome only with the Name of those—strong—stupifying—adulterated—debauch'd—Liquors. After she had supp'd, we took our Leaves; but had the Honour to receive an Invitation to dine with her the Week following; and said, she hop'd there was no need to

make

make Apologies for our not eating with her then; as being Persons of hail Constitutions, those Evening-Refreshments were needless; and made no doubt but that we had already learnt to know, that when Nature is arriv'd to its full Growth, and no visible Signs of Decay, those superfluous Nourishments serve not only to create or increase the ill Humours in the Body, but to raise and cherish ill Dispositions in the Mind.

Amongst the Failings that attend this Lady, and indeed several others of our Sex, this one seems most predominant, through a mistaken Zeal to Vertue; they make too curious Search into those Things they would appear to have the greatest Abhorrence to; which I shall discover more particularly hereafter, and is what every truly vertuous Woman ought to overlook, and endeavour to keep herself in Ignorance of; but perhaps they agree with those Words Mr. *Dryden* makes *Lucifer* speak in his State of Innocence:

For to know Good, is good, and therefore fit;
And to know Ill, is good, for shunning it.

No Doubt but these Words were very proper for his Design, and, amongst others of that Nature, had their desir'd Effect; but, on the contrary, as to the latter Part, were I capable to judge or advise, believe it more safe, as much as possible to remain unknowing of all Things that tend to Ill.

Having been a little indispos'd the last Week, I had the Honour to receive Visits from several of my Acquaintance, most of them being Persons of Distinction and Merit, who, besides the Pleasure they gave me in their Conversations, has encourag'd me to entertain a little better Opinion of my self than ordinary, as finding I am not wholly neglected; I mean by those of my own Sex.

After the first Complements ended, and the Ladies plac'd according to their several Degrees, *Lady Quicksight* broke Silence; *Madam,* said she, *if it won't be impertinent in me to entertain your Company, I'll tell you an Observation I made just now coming through the* Mall. I answer'd, *Your Ladyship will lay me under a particular Obligation, in doing it in a much more agreeable Manner than I am capable of.* She made a Return I did not deserve, and went on, *I suppose you know, or at least have heard of such a Gentleman,* naming him, *a Great Statesman, tho' not so particularly address'd address'd to in this present Parliament, as that before the late Revolution in the Ministry.* I observ'd him in a very pensive Mood, taking several short Turns in the Park, and was as often met by a Nurse with four or five Children, who miss'd no Opportunity of dropping him Curtsies, but was pass'd by a long Time disregarded. At last she bethought herself of another Stratagem, and order'd the Children so as to meet him in a full Body, and attack him by way of Complement, while she lead up the Rear. This unusual Salutation call'd him from his politick Contemplations. He saw them very pretty, and well dress'd, and was extreamly pleas'd with their Manner of accosting him. He ask'd the Nurse if she belong'd to them, and said, he never saw such fine Children in his Life; and imagining their Parents to be considerable, desir'd to know whose they were. The Nurse answer'd, Sir, they are your own, and live in the same House with you. Are they so? *says the Father:* Indeed I did not know it, nor do I remember I ever saw one of them before. But however, to let the Nurse see he did not disbelieve what she told him, and that he approv'd of her Manner of Discipline, gave her a Guinea, and order'd her to take them Home. It's very strange to me, continu'd Lady *Quicksight,* that a Gentleman, who is both a good Husband,

band, and a good Father, and makes it his Endeavour to raise great Fortunes for his Children, should be so extreamly bigotted to publick Affairs, as to remain thus ignorant of his domestick ones, and not know his own Children, tho' they live in the House with him. Not at all, reply'd Delamine; I think it sufficient if he knows his Wife, and converses with her. I know a certain Colonel of the Guards, of City Extraction, but having a natural Inclination to what he calls Gallantry, went two or three Campaigns into Flanders, in Pursuit of Honour, 'till he lost that little he had; and at last came Home, and purchas'd the Commission he is now possess'd of. This Spark has a Wife and two Children, whom he has made such Strangers to him, that he has now almost brought himself to believe there is no such People in the World; and I believe scarce knows any one of them when he meets them; but if by Chance any of his more considerate Companions would be reminding him, he swears it's all Imposition; and knowing the Disadvantages he has reduc'd them to, hopes, that he has hitherto bully'd them out of a just Maintenance, makes no Doubt in a little Time but to bully them out of their just Claim too, without giving any sufficient Reasons for what he says or does. Certainly such a Man must needs be esteem'd heroick, who

can

can thus bravely contend, and triumph over a weak Woman and young Children, becauſe he has put it out of their Power to defend themſelves! and if he gains his Ends, I deſire we may all petition the Parliament to have him publickly acknowledg'd, and treated as a victorious Conqueror. Delamine would have proceeded farther, but the whole Company unanimouſly begg'd her to lay aſide that Subject, he being the common Theme of Diſcourſe for that, or ſomething equally as ridiculous; tho' at the ſame Time all own'd he had once been a very pretty Fellow, and ſo might have continu'd, if he had not took thoſe Methods to make himſelf deſpis'd by all the rational World. While they were thus buſy in Remarks on others, ſtriving who ſhould be moſt heard, I thought it better Manners to give Attention to, than intercept their Talk, 'till at laſt they told me I had not ſpoke two Words ſince they came into the Room. I anſwer'd, that being conſcious of my own Incapacities, together with a due Regard to thoſe who honour'd me with their Preſence, was certain I could reap much more Advantage by being a Hearer, than a Speaker. However, rather than give any Diſguſt by my Silence, I'll venture to draw a Cenſure of a contrary Nature; and for want of ſomething more agreeable,

greeable, shall tell a very odd Thing that lately happen'd to my self, and is one Cause of my present Indisposition. The Ladies all begg'd to hear that, and Lady *Quick-sight* cry'd, *I hope you are not in Love; I never thought you inclining to that Distemper.* Not at all, Madam, said I. Your Ladyship's much more discerning, than the vain Coxcomb that misconstructed me; tho' upon hearing my Story, perhaps you'll say I had as great a Share of Vanity, as he. *You must know here is a Gentleman come to lodge in our Neighbourhood, who takes all Opportunities to let me understand he is resolv'd to keep a very strict Survey over my Actions and Behaviours; so that I am under the greatest Restraints imaginable, to find that I can't stir Abroad, move in my own Apartment, or receive Company, but he must have immediate Information; and is so perpetually lolling in his Window, with his Eyes fix'd here, that it's impossible for any Thing to slip his Knowledge. As to my self, there is nothing worth remarking; but what perplexes me, is poor* Amelia. *She had appointed to call on me for the Opera; and because we don't duly frequent those Places, she was desirous not to miss any Part of the Entertainment. Having been dress'd in a very great Hurry, she took a sudden Whip from the Coach, to hasten me down Stairs;*

but

but had the Misfortune to drop her Shift at the Door, which hung in her Petticoats, and was design'd to have been left at Home: Upon which, the Spark took upon him to burst out into a downright Laughter, tho' he did what he could to smother it, while her Servant took Care to deliver it into my Maid's Custody. You'll guess, Ladies, at the Shame and Confusion this occasion'd us; which increas'd, when we 'sp'd him at our Backs, as soon as we had taken our Places in the Theatre, where I suppose he diverted himself at the Expence of our Blushes. Amelia has never been here since; and for my own Part, I appear as seldom as possible. And is that the only Cause? says Lady Quicksight. When you first began to speak of your Neighbour, I apprehended something more than all this. I found she would pump it out, and thought it more ingenious to do it voluntarily. That is, Madam, said I, what I am going to tell you: This very Gentleman finding me use all Industry to avoid him, and that it would continue difficult for him to see me any where but at Church, manag'd it so as to be in the same Pew with me every Sunday, and always places himself either next, or over against me, incessantly ogling, and using several irreverent Gestures, which gives me abundance of Uneasiness. If, to prevent being star'd at, I turn my Head *on one Side,* he takes Occasion truly to dash his Foot against mine, with Design to set it right again; so that I am oblig'd to keep my Eyes fix'd on my Fan, or look directly over him to the Parson; which methinks gives me a very old-fashion'd Air; for I have observ'd Ladies of the highest Quality, and in the Royal Chappel it self, don't throw away a Look, or misemploy a Thought that Way, but are at full Liberty to compare *Jewels*, receive and entertain one another with as much Freedom, and as great an Air of Gallantry, as in the Drawing-Room, or a Ball at Court. The only Refuge I have under these Restraints, is kneeling; but I'll assure you, my Spark is more a Gentleman, and better bred, than to kneel at Church, or shew the least Devotion; tho' at the same Time I dare say he would not think it beneath him to adore and prostrate himself at the Feet of an insignificant Mortal, in Hopes by such Means, to draw her to her Ruin, while perhaps he is only despis'd and laugh'd at; which indeed is the just Reward of such Endeavours. When I am to rise, he is officiously offering his Hand, and by that Means gains Opportunity to squeeze mine; and, in short, has made all the Advances imaginable; so that it were impossible for me to suppose him otherwise than a *Lover*, tho' he had not spoke one Word yet; but that pass'd for

want

want of Affurance, *and I ever expected when he would gain Courage enough to make a Declaration of his Paſſion* ; *not that I had the leaſt Inclination to accept his Propoſals, tho' he has a pretty Eſtate, and conſiderable Place under the Government* ; *yet there is no Inchantments lodg'd in his Perſon, ſo as to make him amiable in my Eyes. However, I did not know but he might expect I ſhould take it an Honour* ; *and becauſe I would not ſeem to leſſen his Deſerts, or value my own without Cauſe, I ſtudy'd a long Time for an Anſwer to that imaginary Letter he might ſend me, and contriv'd it ſo as he could not think me imperious or fantaſtical, or that my Refuſal was meant in Affront to him, I thought it beſt to ſay, that a Senſe of my own Imperfections had occaſion'd me to vow Celibacy ſome Time ſince, as knowing I am unworthy to be belov'd. This Letter lay by me ſo long, that I began to deſpair of ever having Uſe for it, and grew a little diſturb'd, leaſt the Product of my Studies ſhould be loſt* : *But one Evening I had Notice, that the Gentleman's Foot-man over the way had brought a Letter, and would deliver it only to my ſelf. Upon firſt hearing, I confeſs I was in twenty Minds, whether to ſend this I had by me, or not* : *At laſt, I found it would be a conſiderable Time before I could accompliſh another, and that I had no more*

to

to do with this, but to seal and direct it, and by that Means gain the Reputation of a Woman of a quick Thought. I took his Letter, said I would step up and read it, and send down an Answer immediately. The Fellow told me very briskly, it did not require an Answer, and was gone before I could say another Word. I suppose he had given those Orders, because he was resolv'd to take no Denial; so retir'd into my Closet, and to my Astonishment read this:

Madam,

IT's with infinite Regret I have prevail'd with my self to disclose a Secret, that I with Reason fear will cause you much Uneasiness; and withal to give you this unwelcome Caution; that is, for your own Sake, I beg you'll endeavour to suppress your growing Passion for me, which has been apparently manifest by those Tremblings and Emotions which naturally seize you at my Approach, and I with so much Pleasure have discern'd: But have the Misfortune, Madam, to be engag'd in an Affair my Friends put me upon, before I had the Honour to know of you. It's a just Consideration of your Merit, that won't suffer me to let you languish under a fruitless Expectation of what may never be in my Power to gratify. I hope you are so

good

good a Christian, as to bear this Disappointment patiently, and be assur'd, that tho' I cannot, yet there is nothing in the World I covet more, than to be

Entirely Yours.

It was a long Time before I could recover from the Surprize this Letter had thrown me into, and was really griev'd to find, that one can't blush for a Fellow's Impudence, but he must misinterpret it to Love. At first I was in the Mind to write, and undeceive the Puppy; but upon Consideration, found I should but lessen my self, and increase his Vanity, by shewing any Regard to it; for the only Way to mortify such Animals, is to scorn and neglect them, and to let the Fool see it was not in his Power to cause me the least Uneasiness. The next Day, being Sunday, *I dress'd my self in the best Cloaths I have, and went to Church with a gayer Air than ordinary; where I had not been long, before I had the Pleasure to find my Opposite had met with a greater Disappointment than my self, and could have laugh'd at his Folly, if I had thought it worth while; but to do Justice on both Sides, I can't say I escap'd altogether unpunish'd for my Pride; for in leaving off my Hood that Day, the Weather being grown cool, I got a very great Cold,*
which

which occasions me to keep my Chamber at this Time. The Ladies fell a laughing at my Amour; and by this Time I suppose were pretty well tir'd, and took their Leaves.

I Shall not undertake to give a circumstantial Account of the unhappy Differences that arose not long after the Marriage, between Sir *Bounce Sparkit* and his Lady: Tho' her Vertue, Beauty, and every Merit, were his chief Inducements to enter into the matrimonial State; yet, through the Instigations of his pretended Friends, and her Enemies, he soon grew to an Indifference, and afterwards to a Neglect, or rather ill Usage, of the only Person in the World that entirely loves, and maintains an inviolable Fidelity to him. Sir *Bounce* is one of those who places his whole Felicity in himself, and does not require the Additions a good Wife is capable of giving, to make his Life easy to him; and as he never takes nor gives Reasons for any Thing, he thought fit not long since to withdraw to a separate Apartment, and devote himself up to Gallantries; while his forsaken Spouse has full Leisure to lament her Unhappiness,

or

or Time and Opportunity, if she pleases, to revenge her Injuries; tho' I believe she never entertain'd a Thought of that Nature; but on the contrary, has made it her utmost Endeavours, if possible, to retrieve her Husband's fleeting Passion: In order to which, she went one Morning to his Chamber, where she found him equipping in a riding Habit, and with all the Sweetness in her Looks, and most obliging Terms imaginable, said she was come to Breakfast with him, and to have the Pleasure of an Hour's Conversation, if he would permit it. He answer'd with a very haughty Air, that she had made Choice of a wrong Time to gain any of his Company, being in Expectation every Moment of a Gentleman to call of him for *Hide-Park*; and that if she would shew him any Marks of her Duty and Prudence, she must immediately retire. The Lady began to be a little inrag'd at her cold Reception, and his Ingratitude; and briskly told him, those Cautions were needless, and that she wish'd he would acquit his Duty, as well as she had done her's: Upon this, Sir *Bounce* commanded her not to talk; but she still disobeying, he order'd his Valet to lead her to her own Apartment. This Indignity was resented to the last Degree; and she did not fail to tell him at parting,

It

It is not long since you would have gone down on both Knees, to have obtain'd the Blessing your self. Under this new Discouragement, she flies to *Olympa*, a young Lady, her near Relation and Confident, who lives with her in the House. It's to her only she opens all her Grievances. *Olympa* always endeavours to rally her out of her Melancholy, and tells her, a Husband's Love is not worth preserving; and as she is a true Coquet, declares she can never value any Man farther, than to have the Glory of a Conquest; of which she is so extreamly covetous, that she can't bear the Thoughts of a Cavalier, who is not her profess'd Adorer; and never fails to play the Tyrant, after she has once gain'd a Captive. She will needs have Lady *Sparkit* Abroad to divert her; and being in the Morning, and not in an Humour to dress, they walk'd in Dissabil, to make Choice of some Things they had Occasion for at a Miliner's in the *Pall-Mall*; where, after they had been some Time, were returning Home to Dinner, when *Olympa*, whose Eyes are always open to gay Appearances, 'spy'd a fine young Gentleman with his Head laid down to sleep in a Tavern Window; the Sash being up, and another standing by with a Whip under his Arm. Upon which, she cry'd, *Look, my Dear, do you know either*

ther of those pretty Fellows? Lady *Sparkit* immediately recollected she saw her Husband put on that fine lac'd Coat to ride out in the Morning, and that this other was the Friend he expected should call of him; so concluded they were now come back, and would dine there together. While her Thoughts were thus employ'd, he that stood, gave the other a Pluck, who soon wak'd, look'd upon them, and smil'd. They both saw very plain, at that Time, it was Sir *Bounce* himself; and his Lady was not a little reviv'd at the pleasant Look he had given her, and began to think it was not impossible but that his Mind might now change, as much as it had done before. But however, least her too curious Observation might give any Umbrage, she was going in all Haste; but *Olympa* having an Inclination to look back, saw him beckon, and make all the Signs he could to have them stop, 'till he was ready to throw himself out of the Window. She was extreamly pleas'd with his seeming Eagerness to join Companies, and had already doom'd the Stranger her Slave. She tells Lady *Sparkit*, that she is confident Sir *Bounce* is grown impatient to come to a Reconciliation; and because she would not seem to have any Designs, tells her, she has now a fair Opportunity to close

F with

with her Happiness; which, if loft, may never be retriev'd; and that as it is her Husband who makes this preſſing Invitation, ſhe ought not to ſtand upon Decorums, or raiſe any Objections againſt the Decency of the Place; eſpecially ſince ſhe knew him to be a Man of that Temper whom nothing can oblige, but an entire Obedience and Reſignation to his Will and Pleaſure, tho' it appear never ſo unreaſonable to the World. Lady *Sparkit* was very inclinable to comply with thoſe Reaſonings, but again fear'd his Deſigns might not be ſo well, perhaps, as they at firſt imagin'd. While ſhe remain'd thus dubious, and ſlowly moving homewards, *Philaret*, which was the young Stranger, purſu'd and overtook them, who only bow'd, and offer'd her his Hand to lead them back, without ſaying one Word. She aſk'd why Mr. *Sparkit* would not rather come himſelf? He anſwer'd, *Madam, I very difficultly prevail'd upon him to permit me the Honour.* By the Way, ſhe proceeded to aſk him ſeveral Queſtions concerning the *Park*, and if they had brought any other Company with them. To all which he anſwer'd very *Appropo*. When they were come to the Tavern, ſhe ſaw four or five ſtrange Foot-men ſtand with their Hats off; but thoſe ſhe imagin'd might belong
to

to the Gallant, who was 'squiring her up Stairs, while *Olympa* follow'd. They had not quite ascended, before the other Gentleman came running to meet them; and *Philaret* call'd out, *My Lord* Newlove, *if you were sensible of the Blessing, you would fly to assist me in ushering up these Ladies.* Upon this, they immediately found their Mistake, but too late. *Olympa* run down as fast as she could; but Lady *Sparkit* not having Liberty to get away, clapt hold of the Banisters, and fell into a Swoon. After they had brought her into the Room, they did not fail to use their utmost Care and Diligence to bring her to Life, which was effected in a little Time; but upon finding herself in the Arms of him she had mistook for her Husband, she was ready to fall into a Relapse, had they not convinc'd her by their Behaviours and solemn Protestations, she should remain in their Company with as much Safety, on all Accounts, as with the nearest Relation she had in the World. But all this would not satisfy the disappointed Lady; she intreats, with the greatest Urgency imaginable, to have her Liberty; while they, with an unresisting Air, and most profound Respect, follicit her Stay. By this Time *Olympa* had recover'd her Fright, and was return'd, to make Enquiry of her Friend.

Philaret

Philaret had Notice of it, and with abundance of Arguments and Assurances, prevail'd upon her to honour them with her Company; which she did, in Respect to the other Lady. Lord *Newlove* was so enamour'd with the Beauty, graceful Mein, and modest Carriage of Lady *Sparkit,* whom he stil'd his destin'd Charmer, sent from the Gods to take Possession of a Heart unconquer'd; and that he should esteem himself the most fortunate Man on Earth, if she would permit him to devote it eternally to her Service. Lady *Sparkit* receiv'd these Addresses with all the Coldness and Neglect that's natural to a Mind prepossest; and tho' she had no other Obligations to her Husband, than that of being so, yet she found her Vertue a sufficient Guard against the most powerful Assaults. Lord *Newlove* is a young Nobleman, truly heroick, and grac'd with all the Additions of Art and Nature, which can conspire to make him irresistable; and has so peculiar a Method in making Love, which insensibly steals upon the Hearts of those present, as well as the Person address'd to; and never fails to make her envy'd, tho' it were by a Sister, or Bosom-Friend. In the mean Time, *Philaret,* who is no less deserving, a Relation, and sworn Brother to Lord *Newlove,* entertain'd O-
lympa

lympa with all the Respect and good Manners which becomes a Cavalier to a fine young Lady; yet, tho' she is very desirable, he did not find himself absolutely in Love with her, but kept his Eyes and Thoughts fix'd on Lady *Sparkit*, who always proves most attracting to the real Judges of Perfections. On the other Hand, *Olympa* made him suitable Returns, and was so transported between the Charms she saw in Lord *Newlove*, and that of a Rival's Rage and Resentment, that she had not Leisure to mind the cool Application *Philaret* made to her, which seem'd rather through Restraint, than Inclination: A Treatment she had never been accustom'd to, and what was directly contrary to the Sentiments she had of herself; but finds now, to her great Anxiety, it was not impossible to love, even where she is likely to continue disregarded; the greatest Mortification that can befal a Coquet. As these two Lovers sympathize in all Things, so their Thoughts were equally employ'd on Stratagems to succeed in this new Amour, with that Eagerness to persist, which is always observable in a beginning Flame, both fancying he had the juster Claim, 'till they had quite forgot the Intent of their coming thither, which was to dine with two honest Fellows, who had undergone

gone the Fatigues of a Camp fome Years; one of which was come off with the Lofs of an Eye and an Arm, whom they had accidentally met in *Hide-Park*, from whence they were juft return'd when the Ladies firft faw them, and had already befpoke the Dinner. But now the appointed Time being come, the Brothers of the Blade had difpatch'd their Affairs, and were arm'd: Upon which, they rufh'd into the Room in a moft furprizing Manner; the firft made but one Step up to Lady *Sparkit*, clapt his Hat under his Arm, and cry'd, *My Lord, give me Leave to kifs your Girl*; while the lame one accofted *Olympa* in as familiar a Way. The Ladies being unacquainted with thofe Sort of Salutations, were aftonifh'd at their Manner of proceeding, and were ready to die with the Apprehenfions they receiv'd of them. Lord *Newlove* foon perceiv'd it, and with a becoming Anger, in Regard to the Ladies Prefence, gave Camper a fevere Reprimand for his Infolence, tho' with that Caution as not to put their Reputations in his Power by a Difcovery who they were, but gave them all honourable Affurances of his Protection and Fidelity. By this Time Dinner was come upon the Table, which was with all Magnificence the Place would allow of. It was in vain for the Ladies to

think

think of difengaging themfelves, but on the contrary, were oblig'd to be as fociable as they could. While the Courtiers were employ'd in officiating, and filently admiring, the Soldiers were entertaining the Company with an Account of their military Difcipline, and beg'd they might be permitted to regale them with their martial Mufick; which was refus'd. After Dinner, Lord *Newlove* and *Philaret* approach'd Lady *Sparkit*, with all the Awe and Adoration they would a Deity, from whom they expect their immediate Fate; all which fhe modeftly evaded; while Camper plac'd his Batteries at *Olympa*, and after feveral vigorous Affaults, which prov'd ineffectual, he was conftrain'd to raife the Siege: Upon which, they both retir'd; fo that *Philaret*, in Point of Breeding to *Olympa*, is oblig'd to refign to his powerful Rival, and give him Opportunity for all the Advances that is poffible for fuch an Affailant to gain over a Heart that can't remain wholly infenfible of his Merits; where, in fpite of all her Vertue and Reafon, he fo far prevail'd, as to obtain her Confent for a fecond Meeting; which, though innocently meant, had the Misfortune to be overheard by *Philaret* and *Olympa*, who look'd upon this Adventure to be a Confpiracy againft her univerfal Empire; and tho' before

fore this unlucky Accident, she dearly lov'd Lady *Sparkit*, yet, in the Height of Rage and Resentment, she is ready to sacrifice her to her Revenge, it being entirely in her Power, as she best knows the true Motives of her Husband's Indifference; and that if she fail'd of her desir'd Success in an Attempt projected, she is already assur'd of having him her Vassal, whenever she pleases to command it, tho' the Affection she bore to her Cousin, had hitherto prevented her taking any Advantages of that Nature, but always endeavour'd to conceal it from her Knowledge, that it might not cause her any Disquietude. Lady *Sparkit* is now desirous to be gone, when Lord *Newlove*, who is so transported with the Hopes of future Happiness, is ready to obey her harshest Commands; and together with *Philaret*, conducted them so far as they would permit.

IT's about three or four Months since a very worthy Gentleman, a Member of Parliament, had Occasion to be at a Periwig-maker's Shop in the *Strand*, where he chanc'd to 'spy a fine young Lady alight out of a *Hackney*-Coach from a very handsome Gentleman, to make a Visit to an intimate Friend

Friend of her's, a Country Lady that lodg'd at the next House; he seeing her walk up Stairs, follow'd by her Foot-man, who carry'd several Parcels she had been buying, and came there with Design to have her Friend's Advice in the making up the Cloths for her Marriage, which was to be celebrated the Week following with that young Cavalier who conducted her thither. *Mirtilla*, which was the Country Lady, would needs recommend one *Vainly*, a finical Mantoa-woman that lodg'd up two Pair of Stairs in the same House, and who had made it her Business to insinuate herself into her Favour, to make the Cloths; which *Clarinda* willingly assented to, and gave her Directions accordingly. But to return to our grave Statesman, whom we left in the adjoining Shop, full of Contemplation on the late Angelick Vision. He finds himself all on a Sudden plung'd into a Passion he had never yet experienc'd, at least to such a Degree, tho' almost arriv'd to the Age of Fifty; but since he is so transported with Love, is resolv'd to gratify himself on any Term whatsoever. Accordingly consider'd on Proposals of marrying her with all imaginable Speed; if his Person be not the most amiable, yet his other Qualifications, with the Addition of a great Estate, and Title of Sir *J——*,

J——, he knew were great Inducements to a prudent young Lady, especially if she had no great Fortune, as he wish'd, to make his Address the easier, and begins to think on no Objection, unless that beautiful *Adonis* that came Home with her, as he imagin'd, might prove to be a Lover: But on second Thought, fancy'd so much Resemblance in their Faces, that he concludes them Brother and Sister; so scorning to ask any other Questions than what's the Lady's Name that lodges next Door, he was answer'd *Vainly*, the People not knowing of any other in that House. This was enough for the hasty Lover. He immediately flies into his Chariot, and instead of going to the Play or Coffee-houses, gives Orders to go Home, where he spent the Remainder of that Day and Night in contriving the properest Means to introduce his Passion. Sometimes he is ready to go and throw himself at her Feet; but again considers, that being wholly a Stranger, such an Action might seem too rash and surprizing; and at last concludes on writing first, to beg Leave to wait on her; which he did next Morning in the softest Terms that could be. He acquaints her with his Name, his Rank, his Circumstances; and above all, his mighty Love and indefatigable Resolutions to obtain her for

his

his Wife; is impatient to know when he may be admitted to kiss her Hand; and concludes himself the most submissive, whining Slave, that ever Beauty made so. This was directed for Madam *Vainly* at her Lodging, dispatch'd away in all Haste, and was accordingly deliver'd with a great deal of Ceremony. You may suppose *Vainly* receiv'd all this very civilly, and return'd the Complement as well as she could, with her most humble Service; and that if he pleas'd to take the Pains to come there next Day at Six in the Evening, she would do herself the Honour to attend him. Never was Woman so pleasingly surpriz'd as she, at this welcome Letter. She perus'd it over and over, and fancies every Thing in her Praise, to be substantial Truths; but upon consulting her Looking-Glass more than ordinary, finds herself altogether irresistable, and is ready to fly into a Passion at the rest of the stupify'd World, that could not distinguish her Charms in six and thirty Years Time. She now begins to consider her Admirer; and tho' she never saw him in her Life, yet is extreamly in Love with him for several Reasons. His Quality, Estate, and honourable Intentions to make her great, are powerful Motives; but yet adores him more, if possible, for his penetrating Judgment.

The Title of Ladyſhip, tranſports her to the laſt Degree. She concludes every Thing done, and is the happieſt Woman in the World, in her own Imaginations. She grows eager for the Pleaſure of relating her Conqueſt, and fixes on *Mirtilla* as the propereſt Confident and Adviſer in this Affair. *Mirtilla* was ſomewhat amaz'd, believe me, at the Gentleman's Choice; but however, being a very well-meaning Country Lady, was mightily pleas'd at her Neighbour's good Fortune, in Hopes to have a merry Bout at this Wedding too. She offers her Apartment to receive him, if ſhe likes it better than her own; which was willingly accepted by *Vainly*, who employ'd all her Time in making that, and herſelf fit to entertain ſo conſiderable a Lover; but *Clarinda*, who had really the greateſt Share in the whole Matter, was ignorant of all that paſs'd, and came very innocently next Day to viſit *Mirtilla*, and enquire if her Wedding-Cloths were almoſt finiſh'd, becauſe ſhe had now few Days to turn in. She had no ſooner enter'd the Houſe, but ſhe found the Face of all Things chang'd, only *Mirtilla* was much the ſame Woman as before; but *Vainly* was abſolutely transform'd into another Creature. She had juſt been adorning herſelf to maintain an eternal Conqueſt; ſate playing her

Fan

Fan with the awful Air of some great Lady-Visiter, now and then tuning up her musical Voice to the softest Words she could think on. *Clarinda* was struck all on a Heap in her Thoughts, at this sudden Alteration; but seeing *Vainly* look so very stately, she could not take Courage to ask any Question, nor durst so much as name the Work she expected to have seen done. *Mirtilla* observing her Look surpriz'd and studious, was as much in Pain to have the telling of News, as the other was to hear it; so makes an Excuse to call her into the next Room, where she unfolded the Mystery. *Clarinda* could hardly believe at first Hearing; but *Mirtilla* asserts the Truth with, yea verily, and indeed. This happen'd as *Vainly* wish'd; for she was often upon the Point of bringing of it out herself; but deferr'd, in Hopes *Mirtilla* would save her the Labour. They were no sooner come to her again, but she begins to return her Thanks; for tho' *Clarinda* was a Stranger at present, yet she said she was much pleas'd with her Conversation, and had no Affairs she desir'd might be made a Secret to her, and hop'd they should be better acquainted hereafter; for truly she should very often beg their Companies in her Coach to *Hide-Park*; but indeed she has so many Things to do and
think

think on, that she does not know at which End to begin; and as they are both going to enter into the same Circumstances, she says they must endeavour to assist one another, and make the best Use of their Time. She will needs have *Clarinda*'s Cloths sent away just then to the Mantoa-woman she designs to honour with her Wedding-Garments, and tells her, that in Return, she must make it Part of her Employment to enquire out amongst her Acquaintance for a Lady's Woman, that understands herself and her Business throughly, and knows how to keep due Distance; for she is sure she can never bear a familiar Wretch. But now the Time of Expectation draws near; the Ladies are better bred, than to be interrupting; so take Leave together to spend the Evening at *Clarinda*'s Lodgings. They had not been gone half an Hour, before a fine Chariot and Equipage, with a much more fine Gentleman, stopt at the Door. *Vainly* knew it could be nothing less than her Adorer; runs in all Haste to meet him at the Stairs. After the usual Complements to a Woman of her Appearance, he desir'd to know if Mrs. *Vainly* were at Home: She told him Yes; and that her Name was so. He supposing her to be the Mother, said it was the young Lady he meant, who had done him the Honour to return such and such

such an Answer, upon his taking the Liberty to write to her the Day before. She assur'd him she was the very Person he meant; that there was no other of the Name in that House; and for farther Confirmation, takes the Letter out of her Bosom. He then begg'd ten thousand Pardons, said he was mistaken in the Name; for that Letter was meant to another Lady about such an Age, had such Hair, Eyes, and every Features; and proceeded to describe her very Dress; yet all this was not enough to convince *Vainly*: She did not intend to be so tantaliz'd. She affirm'd she was not above Eighteen, had just such Eyes; and that if he will but come up to the Light, he will find her every Ways as agreeable, if not exceed the other he talks of: But, alas! it was not in the Power of all her Charms and Rhetorick, to draw him one Inch farther. Poor *Vainly* was perfectly confounded at this unexpected Treatment, and Labour lost; and what between Grief, Pride, and Resentment, was ready to break out into loud Complaints, and offer'd to detain him by Force; which oblig'd the mistaken Lover to take very abrupt Leave, extreamly perplex'd at the Disappointment; but not without Hopes that a little more Caution and Industry, may at last bring him to the real

Object

Object of his Admiration: But I understand *Vainly* came pretty even with him afterwards; which I'll refer to some other Paper, when I am better inform'd of that Part of the Story.

FINIS.

Day, most of which, 'tis possible, they would never be wheadled to swallow, were they not so temptingly sweetned with Brevity; in which I confess they very wisely follow the Prescription of a famous Author, who says, that

*———Brevity is allways good,
Tho' 'tis, or is not understood.*   Hud.

Thus too, by not loading their Readers with more Information at once than their Stomachs are able to bear, they have artfully qualified their Labours for the gentler Digestion of the Fair Sex; the *News*, the *Tea* and the *Tatler* having been of late the first things call'd for in a Morning, while perhaps a *Montaign* or a *Seneca*, because they are Volumes, are seldom or never taken up, but after an elegant Meal to lull your fine Gentleman into a Slumber, from which he yawns into his Coach to the *Opera*, where only the elaborate Sense of Sound can wake him. By this Method I am afraid my ingenious Cotemporaries will have

THE
TELL-TALE:
OR, THE
Invisible Witness.

THE Ancients were forc'd to infuse their Morals into Mankind with a *Utile Dulci*, but our modern Single-sheet Authors have found out a notable *nostrum* that they never hit upon, *viz. Utile Brevi*, which in this Age of idle Readers has indeed a very wholsome Effect, as may be seen from the Number of printed Papers the good and bad People of *England* take before Breakfast every Day;

THE TELL-TALE;

OR THE Invisible Witness:

Being the SECRET OBSERVATIONS OF PHILOLOGUS, Upon the Private Actions of Human Life.

To be continued at Leisure.

The FIRST PART.
Of Lovers, and Persons of modern Pleasure.

Infert se septus nebulâ (mirabile dictu)
Per medios, miscetque viris, neque cernitur ulli.
Virg.

Turpe quid ausurus, te sine teste, time.   Mart.

LONDON:

Printed for *A. Baldwin* in *Warwick Lane*; and sold by Mr. *Graves*, next *White*'s Chocolate-House in St. *James*'s Street. 1711.

(Price 1 s.)

Bibliographical note:

This facsimile has been made from a copy in the Beinecke Library of Yale University (College Pamphlets 1848)

The Tell-Tale

Anonymous

have the better of me, in the Care they have taken to increase their Number of Readers, which daily Experience tells us is easier to be brought about by reducing a Book to a Leaf, than by putting a great many Leaves into a Book. And indeed this Consideration had once like to have prevail'd with me to follow their Example of encouraging the weekly Consumption of Paper; but upon Tryal I found my *Pegasus* too high mettled to trott on in the common Road, or to be pull'd in at every third Column of a half Sheet, and perhaps too resty to go on, when he might be only prick'd forward by the dull Spur of a hasty Bookseller, who might illiterately tell me that the fourth Column of *Advertisements* was his only Neat Produce of my Undertaking. I have therefore ventured to give up all Pretensions to Favour, when I am dull by taking my own Time, and have sent my *Observations* into the World, with as much Life as my Fancy at leisure was able to give them.

And now, that my Readers may know by what strange means I am more intimately let into their Secrets, than the many Persons they may take to be wiser, 'twill be necessary to amaze them with the following Relation.

PHilologus; (for that's my writing Name, as *Captain* is a Bully's fighting one, which we equally take to give our selves an Air of Penetration, whether into the Minds or Midriffs of Mankind) *Philologus* then, one Day in the Month of *June*,—no matter what Year, (for I am resolv'd not to be trap'd in my Chronology) I say, (as I have said twice before) *Philologus* taking a solitary Mornings Walk in *Windsor* Forest, where musing on the ill situation of his Affairs, he too well convinc'd himself, that not only his most insupportable Disquiet, but his greatest Indiscretions were owing to the fair *Millamant's* Treatment of his Passion, which made him disrelish all innocent Pleasures of Life, and neglect the honest means in his Power of defending

fending his moderate Fortune against the Reputation of a Mifmenager. This Reflection made him refolve to write to her once for all, and to paint her Mind with the fame Sincerity he us'd to exprefs his own when he lay at her Feet; wifely prefuming (for he's a mighty natural Philofopher) that next to Satiety, a fubftantial Defpair is the beft Remedy for a wounded Heart, and for fuch *Defpair* he cou'd never *Hope*, but from fuch an unpardonable Provocation. You'll eafily fuppofe, from the oddnefs of this Paradox, that the Lady was a Coquet, and the poor Man's unfortunate Defigns were honourable. With thefe Thoughts he fat him down under the Shelter of an old decaying Oak, whofe faplefs Root was forfaken by the mouldring Earth, that fell from it into a fmall Gravel-Pit beneath. Here unfeen, and penfive, he pull'd out his Tablets, and compos'd the following Panegyrick for his faithlefs Fair One.

" I find I have lov'd you better, than
" any of my Rivals, by your ufing none
" of

"of them so ill as my self. You seem
"to place your highest Happiness in the
"Power of your Beauty; and I now
"hope to disturb that Happiness, by
"destroying your Power over me; since
"it seems so much below a Woman of
"your Spirit to have a sincere Re-
"gard for any one Man, I wou'd have
"my Honesty provoke you to hate me,
"that I may from thence strengthen my
"Reason to contemn you, and I believe
"I shall succeed; for the more I aspire
"in my Merit, the lower you descend
"in your Ingratitude. My Affection
"makes you vain; my Sincerity, de-
"ceitful; my Humility, insolent; my
"tenderest Jealousies, guiltily reveng-
"ful: But know, Mrs. *Whatd'yecallum*,
"'tis possible the familiarity of that Ex-
"pression now may make you call me
"sawcy Puppy — not unlikely — I cant
"blame you — But still I say, Mrs. —
"pshaw! I forget your Name — I say
"my Reason is all this while proving
"you more a Fool than a Sharper in
"your Conduct; nay, and so great a
Fool,

"Fool, that I now plainly see 'twas
"only the Wantoneſs of your Eye that
"firſt ſeduc'd my weak Fancy to think
"you handſom; for every wiſe and mo-
"deſt Woman knows all Love, that is
"not cordially ſincere, is ſenſual, ſcan-
"dalous, momentary and inſipid — but
"much good may it do you — you
"like it your own way — and the
"Taſte is not out of faſhion, I own —
"But now I have reduc'd you to this
"ordinary Creature, 'tis time to take
"my Leave of you — I forgive you
"the almoſt irreparable Injury I have
"done *my ſelf* in throwing away ſo
"much of my precious Time after you:
"But don't let what I have ſaid change
"one Tittle of your Smiles or Princi-
"ples — Glance on, that I may find my
"Cure in ſeeing others dye for you; I
"ſhall be no loſs to you I dare ſwear;
"the Weather is as warm as your Youth;
"and you may now venture to leave
"off a Lover like your Tippet, with-
"out catching Cold or Scandal. If I
"ſhou'd relapſe into a Deſire of ever

B "ſeeing

" seeing you again, I hope you will
" have Pride enough not to be at home;
" for after this insolent Epistle, you
" ought to be inexorably out of Hu-
" mour with

Your Horrid Humble Servant
PHILOLOGUS.

 Having finish'd his Billet, he laid his Hand on a Cleft in the Tree, to raise himself from his Seat; but Age had so decay'd its Trunk, that his weight tore out a large Rib from its side, and threw him backwards with the Fracture, which was follow'd with a distressful Groan, and an almost suffocating Smell of Sulphur: This struck him with Amazement, which was yet encreas'd when he perceiv'd from the Gap in the Tree a beauteous Form of Innocence, exceeding all that's human, kneeling with lifted Hands and Eyes before him, which to relieve his Wonder, instantly address'd him in these Words,

 " O blessed Mortal! thrice, thrice
" thrice happy be the Hand that thus

The Invisible Witness.

"restores me to respiring Air, and long,
"long sigh'd for Liberty! Start not,
"nor think that Evil lurks in this illu-
"sive Form; for I am gentle as the
"tendrest Sighs of Infant Love, secret
"as the Pale-cheekt Virgin's Wish, and
"constant as the returning Beams of the
"diurnal Sun, whose fiery Globe has
"thrice full fifty times roll'd round his
"annual Course, since first these airy
"Limbs were by infernal Magick charm'd
"within this knotted Oak: In brief,
"my Name is *Philadel*, by Fate reserv'd
"to be the grateful *Genius* of whatso-
"ever Hand shou'd happily release me.
"My intellectual Fortune past, a time
"more fit shall tell thee; mean while,
"in proof of my extensive Power, my
"Care and will to guard thee, I'll free
"thy injur'd Heart from Love's ungrate-
"ful Chain. That Letter in thy Hand,
"without my Aid, had prov'd thy Ru-
"ine; for Reason's but a weak Defence
"against the insidious Eyes and Arts of
"close resenting Beauty: But I'll unra-
"vel all the ungrateful fair one's Heart,

"and

"and set her naked Soul this Instant
"'fore thy Eyes.

At this the Spirit breathed a circling Cloud of Perfume round his Head, so exquisitely fragrant, it seem'd a blended Quintessence of vernal Odours.

" Thou'rt now, said he, like me,
" *Invisible* to other mortal Eyes; recline
" thy Arms upon my tender Pinions,
" and be convinc'd it is thy Genius
" guides thee.

No sooner had *Philologus* touch'd his Wings, but in a moment, swift as Thought can travel, he found himself whirl'd through the Air, and gently set down in the fair *Millamanis* Apartment, in *Golden Square*; where, to his no great Amazement, he discover'd her in the very Act of Coquetting with Collonel *Sinecure*, who was then, *Philologus* included, her fifteenth Coxcomb in waiting.

By this time, loving Reader, I flatter my self you are in haste to know what sort of Conversation was then passing between this Favourite Collonel and the
Lady:

Lady: But having thus inform'd you by what means I am become Master of this *Invisible Surtout*, 'twill here be proper first to prepare your Expectation, by letting you know what use I do Not design to make of it.

First then, tho' I have the active Secrets of all Mankind in my Power, and shall probably pass a great part of my Time in the most inaccessible Privacies of the fair Sex; yet I can't refuse the Ladies my Word of Honour never to make any of 'em blush by discovering the least Mole or Mark of their Persons, tho' I foresee several of the Fine-limb'd Coquets will endeavour to bribe me to it. In the next place, if any Lady under the unfortunate Disrelish of a Husband, shou'd be frail enough to make a secret Alienation of her Person, or a tender-hearted Virgin (for let 'em be never so modest, sometimes Men will push things to a strange Freedom) shou'd be deluded into the Disposal of her unguarded Premisses, for the uncertain Rack Rent of a Rover's Fidelity, I repeat

peat my Word never to say any thing of the matter: For tho' the World is well bred enough to wink at such venial Slips, while they are only publish'd in a Whisper; yet who knows on what part of their fair Bodies a passionate Gentleman might mark his Resentment, were he to read the private Diversions of his Wife or Sister in a Pamphlet? To undeceive a Man in such a Case, is in my Opinion the next Crime to doing him the Injury: But (as inimitable *Shakespear* says)

He that is Robb'd, not Wanting what is stoll'n Let him not Know it, he's not robb'd at all.

Of all Murthers, that of assassinating the Life of our Reputation seems to me the most barbarous, and an anonymous Author, who has the Fame of the Innocent as well as Guilty in his Power, shou'd expect no more Mercy than he shews. With this negative Merit I hope the Ladies will sometimes do my Labours the Honour to let 'em lie upon their

their Toiletts; where if I can't divert 'em, they may at leaſt, like other vain Endeavours to move 'em, ſerve to pin up their Hair.

When I had writ thus far, I was at a Gentleman's Houſe in *Bedfordſhire*, where there were ſome young Ladies from *London* that came to paſs the Summer with his Daughters; at the ſame time there was a dapper Spark, who the Winter before was a Fellow-Commoner at *Cambridge*, and had ſince taken his *Wits Degree* at *Will*'s Coffee-Houſe, by joyning in the Chorus of Laughers at *Tom Titt*, for his *Stentrophonick* Burleſque of the *Italian* manner of ſinging. This very near fine Gentleman I found was receiv'd in this Family as an honourable Lover of Mrs. *Lucy*. Upon the Strength of which Intereſt he came one Morning uninvited, in his fine Gown and Slippers, to her Tea-Table, while I was making theſe Ladies a private Confidance of my preſent Undertaking; and having read to them to the laſt above Period, I receiv'd (for ought any

any of my Readers know) the Thanks of the whole Company for my Entertainment, which (having chiefly calculated this part of my Work for the Meridian of their Taste and Understanding) gave me a very natural Encouragement to proceed. But, wou'd you beleive it, gentle Reader? no sooner was my Back turn'd, but this invidious Animal, the Wit, whether he thought to recommend his own Parts by it, or was a little musty at Mrs. *Lucy*'s particular Approbation of my Papers, I know not; but this unkind wise Man, taking the Advantage of my Absence, falls foul upon the main Body of my Design, says it was all Invention, and brings down his whole unmerciful Artillery of Logick to prove that my Assertion of having the *Invisible Surtout* was a meer poetical Whimsy, and a Contradiction to all Sense and Nature.——A disobliging Puppy! not but I am pretty even with him, for Mrs. *Lucy* has since declar'd she will never have him upon't. But (as I since told the Ladies) it's no wonder a Fellow, who publickly

publickly professes he does not believe any thing of Ghosts, nor Spirits, nor Fairies, nor — Nay, that most unconversably insists in ill-manner'd Opposition to the whole Family's Opinion, that even *Dreams* are of no signification. I say it's no wonder such censorious People are for destroying any Belief that's harmless and pretty; I therefore hope Mrs. *Methought* and her good Cousins will not question the Truth of a thing that they now see is so plainly in print, to confute him. So without regard to his Malice, I shall e'en go on with the rest of my true Story, and return to *Millamant*'s Apartment, where we left *Philologus* invisibly dropt into her private Conversation with the Collonel.

But here, Ladies, it will be proper to let you know that *Millamant* is that subtle sort of Coquette, who is more tender of her Reputation among the Women than the Men, well-knowing that too streight-lac'd a Virtue among our modern fine Gentlemen is no Bait for a Crowd of Admirers. From this seeming

ing Prudence she is well receiv'd in the greatest Circles; nor shall you in any Company ever observe her transgress the Bounds of an agreeable Freedom with the prettiest Fellow that undertakes her; but the Minute she gets him alone she is sure to throw off the Mask, and while she makes him the flatter'd *Confident* of what she calls her *Rogueries,* she sooths his Vanity from so agreable a Trust, to make the very loosenefs of her Soul the resistless Reason of his Inclination.

In this sort of Intimacy the invisible *Philologus* found her with the Collonel, who was standing with both his Hands clinch'd in hers, toying before the Glass Pannel, to which she often turn'd her Face from him, as affecting an Insensibility of his warmest Vows, but in reality did it to adjust her Charms, and observe unseen the secret Sincerity that then was sparkling at his Eyes. This unforbidding Air encourag'd him to forward his Approaches, by offering her a thousand humble Conditions for a single Kiss, which the unoffended Fair One only

only refus'd by breaking into a silent Smile of Contempt in his Face.—The inapprehensive *Inamorato* ask'd her what she laugh'd at?—*Why, thou silly Wretch,* (said she) *art not thou uneasy enough already? Don't you see I have a malicious mind you shou'd like me: And why will you ask a thing, that to my Knowledge will but put it more into my Power to use you ill?*—O thou insolent, agreeable — Devil, (reply'd the Soul-shot Lover) *this soft Enchantment is not to be born.*—Then trembling in a submissive faultring Voice, he begg'd in Pity of his longing Heart, she wou'd endure what only cou'd relieve him.—*O fye!* reply'd the artful Syren, lifting up her lovely Eyes; then of a sudden dropping 'em into a modest yielding Softness, she muster'd all the thousand darting *Cupids* on her Lips, and stood passive to receive him.——— But here the Scene grew too provoking, nor could the weak Indifference of a half-heal'd Lover support it without a mortal Pang. The careful *Philadel* too foreknowing that the amorous Intimacies to follow, would but more distract the unhappy *Philologus*, snatch'd him on a sudden to his own Apartment in *Bow-street*, where after he had a little reflected on the unfortunate Follies of his Heart, the gentle Spirit soon recover'd him into Reason, and confirm'd him in a manly Contempt of her Infidelity. But because, said he, the Inquietudes that rise from Disappointments of this nature are perhaps as often owing to the Lover's secret Pride as injur'd Inclination, I think it not amiss to give your Resentment the natural Relief of reproaching her. The Farewel Letter you had written to her in the Forest may now be safely sent her, and, to compleat your Cure, be once more invisibly present at her reading of it. Upon this Advice the Epistle, for the better Air of Contempt, was immediately dispatch'd by *Harry*, or *Bell* the Chairman, (I wo'n't be positive which) and *Philadel* with *Philologus* accordingly took their invisible Posts. Just before the Letter came, the *Collonel* had taken his

Leave,

The Invisible Witness. 21

Leave, and left her in all the Gayety of a consummate Satisfaction at her new Conquest; in which Female good Humour her Woman brings her *Philologus*'s Billet, and told her the Man said it requir'd no Answer. This unexpected Message with it gave her some Impatience to open it. There's nothing can better paint her Surprize and Resentment, than her own literal Interjections as she read it. At the first two Lines she smil'd only, with a—*Humh!*—then in a little higher Tone to a — *Hah!* — then reads on, —um,—um,—um,— My Reasons to contemn you —*Soh!* (a little nettled) —um, —um, —Call me sawcy Puppy——*Blockhead!* (vext)— um,—um,—um,— Forget your Name, *Fool!* (stung) — um, — um, —— Reduc'd to this ordinary Creature——*Wretch!* (provok'd) — um, — um, —um, ——— Horrid humble Servant, ——— *Fellow!* (downright intemperate) For here she tore the Letter into as many pieces as if it had been the Heart of her insolent Offender. Then

taking

taking several unsizeable dumb Steps cross the Room, she knit her fine Brow, and set her Ivory Teeth in so intent a Rumination of Revenge, that she gave her Favourite *Veny* a disobliging kick on the Belly for its unseasonable Fondness, and made the poor Creature yelp down Stairs in very near the complaining recitative of a Modern *Italian* Hero. Her Woman alarm'd at the lamentable acromatick Notes, ran to its Assistance, but was accosted at the Door with a Here! You! Idiot! Take that squawling Beast out of my Hearing, and let me never see either of your odious Faces again.——Go!———'Tis impossible to express the Relief *Philologus* receiv'd at her delicious Disorder: (for Lovers, where they can't give Pleasure, naturally descend into the low Desire of giving Pain.) But the subtle *Millamant* having at last weather'd this Storm of her disappointed Pride, seem'd wholly settled into wiser Resolutions, having too much Reason to fear her Eyes had lost their usual Power of punishing the Man, who cou'd cou'd with such unmov'd Defiance dare their worst Resentment; therefore to *secure* her Revenge, she rather chose to wear the *Syren* than the *Harpy*, and on second Thoughts writ to *Philologus* the following Billet.

"*Offended Sir*,
"I am now convinc'd no angry Man
"alive has a better Talent at Re-
"proaches than your self; but are you
"really very wise in making so keen a
"Use of it? when you know in your
"yielding Heart you can't help loving
"me. I grant you, 'tis intolerably
"insolent in me to say so; but what
"then? Is not it true? True, *Philolo-*
"*gus*! Well, well! Don't pout so,
"and I will own I have been a little
"naughty; but you are a little hasty
"too, Mr. *Wisdom*; for if you found
"that Flattery so well succeeded with
"me, why wou'd not you make use of
"it? How cou'd you be so churlish to
"turn my poor dear Vanity Abroad,
"to feed on other Peoples Praises?
"You

" You know I love at my Soul to be
" thought defirable, and is it such a
" mighty Fault to hear from twenty o-
" ther Mouths, that you are in the
" Right for loving me with so much
" Tenderness, and consequently, that
" I am not vain in believing you?
" Have I done any thing that I did not
" always tell you I could not help do-
" ing? And why should you insist so
" hard upon my abandoning the dearest
" Pleasure of my Life, by working
" your self up to a Resolution (as you
" tell me) of destroying it? Well! if
" I must be moap'd up into Prudery,
" I will be flatter'd into it, that's posi-
" tive, and you *shall* own you still
" love me, if possible, more than ever.
" ——Come then,——Be better humour'd
" at five this Afternoon, and throw a-
" way these idle artificial Fears, which
" I shall only punish by what I can't
" help, a little laughing at your being
" so merrily serious with

MILLAMANT.

P. S.

The Invisible Witness.

P. ―. *Don't forget my Snuff, and bring*
* Bianca Man *with you.*

* An Opera Sng.

No sooner had she finisht this Letter, but *Philologus*, who overlook'd her as she writ it, found all his weak Resentment, and hardest Thoughts of her Ingratitude, dissolve; his fond forgiving Heart again took Fire, and call'd his very Eyes in Question; nor could he think but her late Reception of the Collonel was the Effect of *Philadel*'s officious Care, and all Illusion. And indeed, what might not a Resentment so artfully suppress'd, a Submission so affectedly affected, and a secret Inclination so slyly insinuated through her whole Letter, have wrought upon an open amorous Heart? But as she was folding it up, he soon, alas! resum'd his disappointed Thoughts, and heard her smiling thus confess the *Syren*, ――― *O silly, silly Wretches!*

Wretches! (said the Revenge-indulging Charmer) *to think their manly Senſe can lead or alter us? How eaſily a half-kind Word or Look can baffle their Reſentment? Indeed* Philologus, *you'll pay moſt dearly for your Inſolence! Don't I know thy poor weak Side? And unleſs ſome Accident disfigures me, I will uſe thee without Mercy; and when thou'rt on the Rack, I'll make thy pretty tortur'd Heart confeſs I am moſt barbarouſly handſome.* This Soliloquy was uttered with ſo calm an Air of inward Satisfaction, that the impatient *Philologus* deſir'd *Philadel* immediately, to withdraw him to his Lodgings, where not long arriv'd, he received the above Letter from *Millamant,* which he return'd by the ſame Meſſenger, incloſ'd in a Blank, and unopen'd. I ſhall not tire the Reader with her ſingular manner of receiving it, nor of her many other fruitleſs Endeavours to recover him, *Philologus* having yet kept his Reſolution, to be never more viſible in her Company.

Yet *Philadel,* who knew the Weakneſs of a reſolving Lover, notwithſtanding omit-

omitted no Opportunity of letting *Philologus* into her moſt diſſolute Privacies, not only to divert the naturally returning Images of her agreeable, and ſometimes reſiſtleſs Converſation paſt, but as much to rivet in his Mind the utter Impoſſibility of her ever making an honeſt Man ſincerely happy: And as from the Depravity of human Nature Men alleviate their Griefs by ſeeing others ſuffer in the ſame Misfortunes, *Philadel* judg'd it proper to let *Philologus* ſee he was not the only melancholy Fool of Mrs. *Millamants* making: I therefore hope the very different Actions that attend the reſt of her Hiſtory, will excuſe my purſuing it ev'n to her matrimonial Cataſtrophe, which I propoſe will be thought as ridiculous as extravagant, yet not more extravagant than true.

Among the Crowd of her Admirers, no one was leſs ſuſpected her Lover than *Robin Rough*, ſuch was his *Nomme de Guerre*, which from the honeſt Downrightneſs of his Temper, he ſtill kept ev'n after his Acceffion to a fair Eftate, and Title.

This Gentleman being a Match of her Relations propofing, had (I might fay confequently) the Misfortune of being diftinguifht with her Averfion, at firft Sight; for 'tis the nature of a Coquet to be utterly fpontaneous in her Favours; the leaft Hint of Advice or friendly Direction, infringes her Liberty of pleafing her Fancy, and confequently juftifies her unlimited Refiftance of the arbitrary Government of Reafon: But however, *Millamant* lov'd to be merry and wife; and it appearing that this Rough Sir *Robert* was of the *Male Sex*, that was found fufficient Merit to qualify him for a Lover; and the worft Lover, in the modern Senfe of a fine Lady, is too good to be loft for want of Encouragement; fo that we are not to be furpriz'd, if when fhe found his honeft Pride would not bite like every greedy Coxcomb at a common Bait, fhe fign'd ev'n to a Blank of kind Conceffions, to engage him; not But fhe was otherwife a prudent Manager

Manager of her Favours, and never advanc'd more to any Man, than he had Spirit enough sincerely to long for, or was absolutely necessary for the Subsistance of his fruitless Passion: And since every Lover has not the same Modesty of Appetite, a *Coquet* (whose Life is miserable without Lovers) must submit to the different Demands of their Sense, Humour, Quality or Complexion to secure 'em: Some gentle Sighers perhaps will surrender upon the bare Summons of common Civility; this demands a Hand, a Smile and a Whisper, that the Liberty of writing only, *Philologus* submitted upon her condescending to answer his Billets. The Collonel held out till he was shot through the Heart with a Kiss; but Sir *Robin* manfully maintain'd his Ground till she had actually sign'd to the more honourable Preliminary of his Passion, which her faithless and unbounded Thirst of Dominion never intended to ratify: Behold then the following Instrument of her Perfidy, and his Undoing, which in an insidious good Humour this fair Treatyty-breaker writ in answer to one of his most tender Remonstrances, of which the invisible *Philologus* took a Copy one Morning, just as *Robin* had read it in his Bed about nine times over.

MILLAMANT *to Sir* ROBERT, &c.

And why this hard Demand upon my Heart? Need I confess in Words, what if you are a Lover, a thousand little Actions might convince you of? Whom do I distinguish with an equal Value? Others may talk to me indeed; but alas! I only think with you: Are you not always nearest me in Assemblies? And whom do I regard when you approach me? Are you not ev'n hated, envyed for the Intimacy I shew you? You cou'd not but observe the sudden Gravity and Discontent that sate in every Face when you came in last Night; and yet the something more than Chearfulness that remain'd in mine upon your Entrance! Did not I in a downright rude Whisper kindly ask you if you had kept your Word in not sending the Subscription Tickets you promis'd that teizing Creature my Lady Never-

The Invisible Witness. 31

Neverfail, *for the new Opera to morrow?* *And a little after reacht over two People for a Pinch of* Brazile, *which you know I hate, only to have a Pretence of leaning my other Hand upon yours? These little Follies, however slight in appearance, give me a thousand Confusions, when I reflect what tender guilty Consequences you may draw from them. Have I not in a more serious Proof too of my Esteem, profess'd I wou'd never alter my Condition but with your Consent: Imagine but how many vain Pretenders wou'd think themselves immoveably secure of me with half the half of such a Confidence? Why will you then so rigorously insist that I shou'd name the Person, who can't be happy but with your Permission? Are you not sure there is but One on Earth you ever can consent to? Why then this pressing Diffidence of my Friendship? Why must the Shame of naming him be mine? Ease me at least of that unnecessary Guilt; you'd think me confident shou'd I plainly tell you what you unkindly know, who 'tis, that only, and for ever can engage the Heart of* MILLAMANT.

This Billet one wou'd think were the last Step to a right Understanding; but mark the unfortunate Use this will-be-wise Gentleman made of it. These Confessions he now thought gave him a Right to regulate her Conduct, and if possible, before he engag'd for ever, to form her Mind as beautiful as her Person; which impracticable Scheme often drew him into the unbred Address of obliging her to hear her Faults, with scarce the Comfort of saying a civil thing to her Features; which intolerable Neglect of her Beauty, rous'd the Lady into a vigorous Assertion of her unquestionable Right of being in the Wrong; and the farther she advanc'd that Principle, the more he found himself piqu'd in Honour to thwart and reduce her; so that their most intimate Conversations in a little time began wholly to be made up of Powts, Huffs, Snubs and studied Contradictions; and under the appearance of this displeasing Behaviour, honest *Robin*, without designing it, had made his secret Pretensions to *Millamant*, utter-

utterly unsuspected by his shorter sighted Rivals, as the Sequel will better inform you.

The Collonel transported with his late Reception at *Millamant*'s, flew to *White*'s, as the nearest *Rendesvous* of idle young Fellows, to unbosom his Happiness; for 'tis the Fate of a Coquet never to have her Favours long a Secret, every flatter'd Pretender having as much Right to boast of his singular Success, as her Vanity has to encourage above one Pretender.

No sooner was the Collonel arriv'd, but the first Person he saw through the Sash, was *Robin*, soberly poring over a News Paper: Upon sight of him he threw himself from his Chariot so hastily, that he scarce staid to swear by the way at the six Inches of his Sword that was snapt in the Coach Door as he got out. Entring, he familiarly twicht the Paper out of his Hand; which *Robin* returning with a dumb Stare of Contempt, the trans-

ported Collonel confounded him with a familiar Kiſs and a Hug, and hurried him into the Garden before he had time to refuſe him; whither upon *Philadel*'s Advice I follow'd him, and in half a Minute found him in the height of an ecſtatick Deſcription of *Millamant*'s Charms, Wit and good Humour, which he concluded with ſwearing that ſince he was born, he never taſted the true Pleaſures of a Woman till within this half Hour; upon which *Robin* gave him a ſtern ſide Look, and by the Fire in his Eyes, ſeem'd to be in doubt whether it might not be proper to knock him down; but his Curioſity overcoming his Reſentment, he at laſt turn'd to him, and ſtroking his Chin, ſaid; "Prithee my dear happy Rogue be a "little more particular, for I have no "Notion that Creature can make "any Man have a better Opinion of "her than I have. What has ſhe ſaid, "and what has ſhe done to thee?
"Done!

"Done! said the other, 'tis impossi-
"ble to tell thee! But imagine all
"that mortal Woman can do to en-
"chant and fix the Soul of a vigo-
"rous, unthinking young Fellow;
"and that she has done to me!
"S'death Sir! (says *Robin* colouring)
"you don't pretend to have layn
"with her; No, no, (reply'd the
"Collonel) if I had, dear *Robin*,
"my Transport wou'd sooner have
"been over; but to tell you the
"Truth, whatever Opinion you may
"have of her, or of me for believing
"it, I am now convinc'd that there
"is not in the World a Woman of
"more Beauty, Innocence, Sinceri-
"ty and agreeable Virtue. And
"prithee dear Collonel, says *Robin*,
"by what Symptoms had she disco-
"ver'd her self to be Mistress of
"these incredible Qualities; for, bar
"her Complexion, I never found
"in all my Observation, that she
"had the least Flavour of any
"of

" of them. Why there's the thing;
" (reply'd the Collonel) your Beha-
" viour to her, and mine, have been
" diametrically oppofite: Your Plain-
" dealing has always fow'rd her Pride
" into a Juftification of more Follies
" than fhe ever was guilty of; and my
" little Complaifance has fweeten'd
" her into a Difcovery of more good
" Qualities than all the *Faux-prudes*
" of her Sex pretend to; and be-
" caufe you infift upon Symptoms,
" I'll be plain with you; I am firft
" convinc'd of her Virtue, by the fe-
" veral fuccefslefs Attacks I have
" made upon't; and of her Under-
" ftanding, by the generous Diftin-
" ction fhe has made of *Me* from the
" reft of the young Coxcombs that
" follow her, whom by the way, you
" may depend upon it, fhe only ad-
" mits for her Diverfion: Then fhe
" has a Softnefs in her Sincerity, that
" exceeds all the Charms of her whole
" Sex blended together. In fhort,
                              " dear

"dear *Robin*, I am so far engag'd, that 'tis impossible to think of retreating or living without her; and therefore, how mad soever you may suppose me, may I perish if I am not seriously resolv'd to marry her.——You may think what you please of Assurance, Importunity, and all that—It's all Stuff—Just so much time lost; for I am now heartily convinc'd that Marriage is the only way in the World I can hope to debauch her."

Robin, whose Looks all this while shew'd the various Resentment of his Heart, had much ado to keep his Temper, but seeming more exasperated at the Conduct of *Millamant* than the Collonel, who had at least the blind Excuse of not thinking he was making Discoveries to a Rival, at last rose up, and as he walk'd off told him, "That all this Story had not in any one Point alter'd his Opinion of the Lady, but this he knew

"knew, that whenever she was ap-
"parently Mistress of those good
"Qualities which he had been so
"privately let into, he was sure the
"Collonel wou'd never be *admitted*
"to marry her———Nay, but pri-
"thee, dear Robin, (says the Collonel, holding him by the Sleeve)
"*why so positive? Blood Sir!* (re-
"ply'd the surly Spark) *I have my*
"*Reasons for it.* ——— At which, in some Heat, he broke from him, brusht in a straight Line through the Company to the Street Door, steps into the first Chair, and being ask'd *where his Honour would please to go?* says never a Word, but with an absent Face continu'd deaf and dumb, 'till the Chairman, despairing of an Answer, cry'd, *Hold up Tom*; which happening just as his Thoughts had roll'd into a Resolution, out walks my Gentleman from the Chair again, with the same insensibility he had enter'd it, and at last broke from the Profundity

fundity of his Silence, by calling haſtily for Pen, Ink and Paper.—The Collonel ſomething alarm'd at his late manner of leaving him, and ſeeing him ſit down to write with ſome Concern in his Looks, imagin'd it not impoſſible but his Billet might conclude in the unſociable Stile of a Challenge, and conſidering that Conduct was as uſeful a Virtue as Courage, wiſely walk'd off, and the ſame Afternoon gallop'd his Hunters to *Epſom*, whence he did not return in four Days, having in that time, by his Side-wind Inquiries, convinc'd his Prudence that *Robin* had no diſagreeable Deſign againſt him.

Robin, who was writing to *Millamant*, had made at leaſt fifteen Beginnings to his Letter, not being able to coin Epithets expreſſive enough for his Reſentment.——His firſt Attempt was to this purpoſe—*Tho' I intend to beat the ſpruce Coxcomb, whom not an Hour ago you, even to a Proſtitution,*

tution, favour'd with your profligate ———This seeming to show him too much concern'd for such a Creature was scratch'd out, and a plain honest Reproach was thought more like a Man of Resolution; as thus, *Heaven has not made you more beautiful than your daily Conduct has contemptible* ——— No! Damn it! Why should he blow up her Pride by allowing her beautiful? He wou'd not have her think he was still so much her Fool, whatever he had been. ———Then on he goes in a fresh Line,———*Since I was once weak enough to love you*——— Consume her! Why should he shew himself so Tame, Passive, &c. ——— Out goes that too. ———No! He would make *her* Life as miserable as she had endeavour'd to render *his*. ——— Soh! Now we have it,— and to't he goes again.———*Tho' your Principles are above Reproof, yet your Actions are within the reach of Punishment, which your*

your *Injurious Treatment* has given me a Right to inflict on you; and may this wrong'd Heart of mine be for ever branded with the Infamy of doating on your Shame, when I forgive the vile abandon'd —— Here pausing for a proper Term, a new Thought caught hold of him, when starting up he cry'd, *Damn her! I wo'n't threaten, but do.* Then crumbling up his unfinish'd Scrawl, he cramms it into his Pocket, and hurries into a Chair to her Lodgings.

'Tis not easy to conceive the Relief *Philologus* found from this poor Man's Sufferings: How plainly this turn'd his Eyes into himself? How often had he been in the same ridiculous Torment? But he now pitied the Rival, whom without this Discovery he might naturally have hated; nor indeed cou'd all the Strength of his Philosophy ever have broke his miserable Chain, had not the supernatural Power of *Philadel* redeem'd him.

him. He therefore hopes, since few Lovers are so immediately under the Care of a *Guardian Genius*, that this Example will be as useful to their Conduct in such unfortunate Amours, as a more elaborate Precept: 'Twas to the want of such a *Genius* that honest *Robin* ow'd the greatest Miseries of Life, into which (his Honesty disdaining to make the least Allowances for his Mistresses Frailties) he was daily and more deeply plunged.——But to follow him to *Millamants*.

Philadel, to omit no Circumstance that might satisfy the Curiosity of *Philologus* took Care to let him be *invisibly* in her Apartment before *Robin*'s Arrival, where he found the Fair One at her Toilet, in an indolent Contemplation of her half-naked Beauties, repeating Verses, and pointing her Arrows for the ensuing Slaughter of the Day. The Weather being warm she only sat in her Petticoat

coat and Shift, which was juft put on, and hung fo loofe upon her Bofom, that it fometimes gave *Philologus* a tranfient View of that Alpine Manfion of her faithlefs Heart; and indeed, to any other Eyes, the Bloom, the Health, the foft unfhaded Luftre of her Charms had been infupportable, but it rather ftruck him into a melancholly Reflection, *viz*. How hard it was upon the fincere part of Mankind, that not the leaft Tincture of her fullied Soul fhould be vifible on its whitenefs; that fuch a calm and Silver Sea fhou'd be unfpotted with a Mark to point us out the fatal Rocks that lurk within its Shallows. But to do Juftice to our Modern Beauties, we find, that to be fair and faithlefs is no new Encroachment upon the Liberties of their fighing Subjects, and tho' it may feem a little unequal, yet it has been always a confiderable Branch of their Prerogative; of which *Horace*, who

44 *The Tell-Tale:* or,

who was an Authentick Wit, and a fine Gentleman, above seventeen hndred Years ago, gives us the following Precedent in one Mrs. *Barine* a Coquet, and a top Toast of the same standing.

> *Ulla si juris tibi pejerati,*
> *Pœna, Barine, nocuisset unquam:*
> *Dente in nigro fieres, vel uno*
>   *Turpior Ungui,*
> *Crederem: sed tu, simul obligâsti*
> *Perfidum votis caput, enitescis*
> *Pulchrior multò, Juvenumq; prodis*
>   *Publica Cura.*

Which till *Robin* comes, Ladies, I desire you will be pleas'd to entertain your selves with in *English*.

If Perjuries cou'd reach thy Face,
 And mark thy Falshood there,
Cou'd I thy smallest Feature find
 Disfigur'd by thy faithless Mind,
Then safely I thy Vows cou'd hear:
        But

The Invisible Witness.

*But thou no sooner art forsworn,
Than in thy Looks new Charms are born,
And when thou mov'st in publick View,
Ten thousand Sighers think thee true.*

Now let us suppose her Woman sticking her last Pin into her Gown, and her Chair at the Door, when we were alarm'd with a Rap! rap! rap! at which Mrs. *Fib* was order'd to scout, and insist upon her being at Home to no Body; but *Robin* (for 'twas he that knock'd) not being us'd to believe any thing sooner than his own Eyes, had already got through the first Lye at the Street Door, and met the second upon the Stairs; which not succeeding, Mrs. *Fib* flew back to her Lady before him, who hastily demanding who it could be she durst own her to, was answer'd, Madam, 'tis Sir *Robert*; I told him positively your Ladyship was not at Home, and he said I ly'd, and—*she tells you true Madam*, said the stern
Baro-

Baronet bouncing in; *I did say she ly'd, and your Ladyship sees I am not mistaken.* At which the Lady (as indeed she had reason) turning about and colouring, told him, that he was yet mistaken if he thought she was to bear such Treatment; that she was only at Home when she pleas'd, and to whom she pleas'd; and he shou'd find she knew what Resentment became her for so unmanner'd an Insult to her Sex and Quality; with which last Words she was making to the Door with full Sail, when *Robin* clapping his Hand upon the Key, whisper'd in her Ear; *By Heaven I won't part with you; and if you don't send your Woman out of the Room, I'll expose you before her.* At this she started back, look'd with a full Frown in his Face, heav'd up her almost bursting Bosom; and when she could hold her balmy Breath no longer, threw open her extended Arms, and lifting up her brillant Eyes to the Powers above, cryed

The Invisible Witness.

cryed out, *By all that's sacred I'll have full Revenge,* then flounc'd into a Chair, and by the nimble Motion of her Heel against the Floor, spoke the dumb Distresses of her quivering Indignation. *Robin* in this Interim of her Silence, by the tip of a Wink, gave Mrs. *Fib* to understand that he was willing to let her out; the Damsel not much caring for quarrelsome Company, march'd of on Tiptoe for fear of disturbing her Lady's Contemplation: The Baronet having lock'd the Door after her, immediately whipt the Key into his Pocket; at which the mute Lady starting up, he press'd her to keep her Seat, and clapping himself down by her, said, " *Have a little Patience, Madam, till* " *I have just begg'd your Pardon for* " *my rude Intrusion upon your Privacy, and I don't question but I shall* " *soon furnish you with a much properer* " *Occasion for your Disorder.*" At this the insulted fair one swell'd again, when

when her intrepid Offender thus proceeded: " I perceive, Madam, by
" your Confusion, you are apprehen-
" sive of the Guilt I am going to re-
" proach you with; and becaufe 'tis
" natural for Women of your Princi-
" ples to perfue with mortal Hate the
" honeft Fool that dares to let you
" know, *He knows* your darkeft Infi-
" delities; I am therefore refolv'd to
" punifh what I can't reclaim, and
" make your Life as miferable by my
" Refentments, as you have made it
" infamous by your Conduct; and
" that I may ftop at nothing in the
" Power of an injur'd honeft Man,
" that may inflame your Averfion to
" me, know, Madam, — Upon my
" Soul Sir, (faid the temperate Lady,
" interrupting him) you give your
" felf a needlefs Trouble; you have
" already fo entirely fucceeded there,
" that my Averfion's ev'n tir'd with
" provoking you; and I'm afraid if
" you don't a little fupport it, it
" will

"will dwindle into a downright, "dumb, indolent Contempt for you. "Look you Madam, (reply'd the "Baronet a little nettled) you need "not snap so at every Occasion to "exasperate my Aversion to you; "the Measure of my Provocations "has long ago been full: But I can't "help telling you, and with some "little Triumph in my Heart, that "your conscious Hate to me is as in- "famous, as mine to you is justifiable "to the World. It's a Sign at least "(said *Millamant* a little warm'd) "that mine's something deeper rooted "in my Heart, since I dare stand the "utmost Censure of the World to "give you my sincerest Demonstrati- "on of it. S'death Madam! (reply'd "the provok'd Gentleman) don't "think to extenuate your Guilt by "insinuating your Aversion as the "Cause of it; no! no! Madam, "that Artifice is too shallow; 'tis not "from Provocation, but by Nature "you

" you are false and poorly spirited; for
" Pride alas! you have none! or you
" wou'd blush and startle at the saw-
" cy Liberties you dayly bear from
" every flattering Coxcomb's fulsome
" Tongue: Resentment you have
" none! For ev'n Revenge, when
" dangerous, you tremble at, and
" are only valiant in Ingratitude:
" Had you the least Tincture of a
" *real* Spirit, your Cheeks wou'd
" burn with red Confusion, to ima-
" gine that this very Day you have
" bestow'd your shameless Favours on
" a Rascal that had not Faith or Sense
" enough to keep 'em a Moment se-
" cret ev'n from his Rival! your Cox-
" comb *Sinecure* I mean, whose Vani-
" ty not an Hour ago was swell'd
" ev'n to bursting, with every inti-
" mate Particular of your transpor-
" ting Conversation!" Here the Lady, partly to provoke him, and partly to gain time for Thought, bursted
into loud Laugh, not yet knowing
whether

The Invisible Witness.

whether she should utterly forswear the Fact, or by an over-acted Confession still keep his Jealousy in doubt; or, in case of the worst, his convinc'd Resentment at Defiance; which last Thought seeming to give a double String to her Bow, was resolv'd on; and in order to it, the Laugh most unmercifully continued; from which at last sinking by Degrees into a setled Face, she made our broiling Lover this provoking Apology. *I vow, Sir, I ask your Pardon; but when I see a Man pretend to despise his Mistress, when his poor jealous Heart is upon the Rack at her every least Favour given to another! ha! ha! I protest it kills me to think how ridiculously his solemn Philosophy becomes him, ha! ha! ha!*

Sir *Rob. Death and Furies! Is't possible! Can you with such Unconcern then own your Perfidy? Confusion!*

Mill. *Own it! O my Soul! How foolishly have I betray'd my self? I find then you only suspected it? Lord!*

how easily might I have deny'd it all this while? I vow I thought you had said the Collonel himself told you the Particulars: I am certainly the most thoughtless Wretch!

Sir Rob. *Distraction!*

Mill. Well, but Sir Robert! *now, you know I am false, pray what am I to be done to? For unless you beat me, I can't imagine what Course you can possibly take to be even with me?*

Sir Rob. *Racks and Daggers!* (Then turning hastily to her) *No Madam! First I'll beat your Favourite Rascal: I'll make him before your guilty Face renounce his impudent Pretensions to you. By all that's brave and daring, I'll make him scandalous to be spoken to.*

Mill. Ay, but how shall I do to like him the less for all this? For how do you know but I have already order'd him to forswear upon all proper Occasions, his having the least Thought of me? And then you know all this noble Fury of your Resentment will seem to suffer a

Non-

Nonsuit——*But you always fancy we Women have no forecast.*

Here the Lover's Heart grew too full to support his Passion and his Injuries; his Anger was now lost in his Amazement; and as his Power of Thought return'd he sunk insensibly into a silent Cordial Sorrow. I saw him, as he walk'd to the Window, draw his Handkerchief to wipe away a Tear that stole upon his Cheek. The Lady in his alter'd Looks discovering the dawn of Victory, took care to push it home, by an immoveable Disregard of his Anguish; when leaning back in her Chair, with Arms indolently stretch'd, and yawning, she cry'd,——*Well! but dear Sir Robert, pray unlock the Door, you know, my Lord, my Uncle is always admitted without asking Questions, and if he should come and*——*Lord! you know, 'twould be mighty ridiculous to see one lock'd here*——*I don't know how!* The patient Lover, quite sunk and

and confounded with her amazing Defence againſt his vain and formidable Reproaches, ſubmiſſively unlock'd the Door; then took two or three reſtleſs Turns acroſs the Room; now ſighing, now ſtopping ſhort and ſtarting, ſometimes throwing in a diſjointed Sentence; when the Lady, to compleat her Triumph, civilly ask'd him if he did not ſeem to have a Mind to ſay ſomething? *Yes, Madam,* (reply'd the tortur'd Wretch) *But where ſhall I begin? How ſhall a Man, rack'd as I am with double Deſpair, expreſs the Anguiſh of his Heart? Or what avails it to complain to one, that wants as well the Power as the Will to yield me a Relief?* — Nay, *Sir,* (ſaid the grave *Millamant*) *if I want the Power indeed* — *Madam* (continued he) *You need not make me a Reply, I am too mortally convinc'd I ſhall never profit by any thing you can ſay to me. When I came hither, I thought to have given you as much painful Shame and Confuſion*

Confusion for your Guilt, as my swollen Heart then felt for your injurious Falshood; but alas! I am mistaken, you have return'd on me the Pains I thought to give, have found the artful means to triumph o'er my weak Reproaches, and victoriously insult me for complaining.—I own my self subdued, but cannot hug my Chain, for I cou'd even part with Life to rid me of my blameful Passion; but when I think the Shame of dying for you will live after me, I ought to endure my Life to expiate my Folly.—And yet, mistake me not, my Disappointments are not so much owing to your Neglect of me as of your self; my Grief is, that you are so exquisitely amiable, so irresistable an Object of Desire, without the least Mark of grateful Virtue to cherish or support it.—Oh! 'tis inexpressibly tormenting to see you daily wear your wanton Heart upon your Eye, which every wandring Glance offers to Sale for new coin'd Vows and Flattery! This, this 'tis that

that heaves my Breast with Sighs, that I have at last discover'd how beautiful a Creature I have lost, that I am curs'd with loving what I can't reclaim, yet might (like other happy Fools) be pleas'd with, did I not love too well.

Here the attentive Lady seem'd to blush with secret Pleasure at his warm Confession of her Beauty, and its Pain-giving Power, which the melancholly Lover perceiving, paus'd a while, then sighing thus proceeded: Good God! Is't possible! That ev'n now you seem more mov'd with my bare Allowance of your Beauty, than all the real Conflicts of my tortur'd Heart? Yet all I have said but grants you the Power of doing immeasurable Wrongs, which without Sincerity of Soul your sensual Beauty never can repair.——— But why do I wast my Words against the Wind? And enter upon Thoughts that stab me with reflected Follies? Farewel! Ungrateful to your self as well as me! I'll do my best to trouble you no more, but if I
find

find it impossible to forget my Injuries, I'll take Care my next Resentment shall be above your Power of insulting it. In the warmth of which last Words, regardless of all Ceremony, he left the Room, without expecting her Reply.

I must confess, the undrest Honesty of his ill-treated Passion wrought me to so sensible a feeling for him, that I desired *Philadel* immediately to withdraw me, lest I might have been a farther Witness of her more deliberate Barbarity.

With this sort of Success had this unhappy Gentleman follow'd the Chace for nigh two Years, every Day yielding him fresh Occasion of some unmerited Uneasiness, or insuppressible Resentment; but his Injuries at last made so strong a Head against his Passion, that the whole View and Bent of his disappointed Heart was turn'd upon Revenge; to compleat which, he subdued himself into a Disguise of his Resentment, and softned the natural

tural Severity of his manner. Thus alter'd in his Behaviour he sometimes contriv'd to meet *Millamant* in a Visit, where he usually appear'd with a well-bred Easiness, that seem'd to allow her less in the wrong, and himself now inclin'd to any moderate Terms of an *Ecclairciſſment*.

In this Situation I left their Affairs without the Curiosity of making either of them an invisible Visit, 'till about two Months after; when one Night in *August* (having finish'd my *Tour* of Observations for the Day) *Philadel* dropt me in St. *James*'s Park, where the silent Solitude, and full Brightness of the Moon, tempted me to walk, and pass an Hour in lonely Contemplation; in which fix'd Amusement my heedless Eye was attracted by an unusual Illumination, in a large House at some distance in *Westminster*. My Curiosity being a little waken'd, I ask'd *Philadel* the Occasion of it, who told me, What was doing within

The Invisible Witness. 59

in wou'd surprize me more than all the Discoveries I had made since my first Entrance into my *invisible State*. This giving me more Impatience, the kind Genius soon reliev'd me, by instantly conveying me to the House, where in the Drawing Room I found about half a Score Persons of both Sexes standing together, and all silent; when of a sudden from the middle of 'em I heard a grave solemn Voice pronouncing the Holy Form of Matrimony; upon this I mov'd forward, imagining that on sight of the happy Couple then in Junction, I shou'd meet with the Surprize that *Philadel* warn'd me of; nor indeed did even the Warning lessen my Amazement, when I beheld the long suffering Sir *Robert* and the beauteous *Millamant* Hand in Hand, before Witnesses at Peace, and quietly plighting an eternal Troth. When the Ceremony was ended, and the Company busied in the usual Complements

plements on that Occasion, I ask'd *Philadel* what Miracle had produc'd this unexpected Union? who told me, Sir *Robert* had lately had another Estate fall'n to him, and that *Millamant*'s chief Dependance being on my Lord —— her Uncle, she durst no longer refuse the pressing Instances his Lordship had made in the Baronet's Behalf, who since the late Addition to his Fortune had generously sollicited his Interest with more Earnestness than before. But is it possible, said I, that Sir *Robert* should be so soon reconcil'd to her intollerable Treatment of his Passion? Have Patience, said *Philadel*, he is now taking the Bride alone into the next Room, follow him, and your Question will be fully answer'd. Here indeed my Curiosity being on Tiptoe, I had no more to say, but immediately took my Post of Observation, when the Bridegroom shutting the Door, entertain'd his fair Help-
Mate

Mate with the following fullness of his *Heart*, *viz.*

Now, *Madam*———*I am*———*your Husband, and what you are remains in my Dispose for Life; your Fortune, Person, and your Freedom all resign'd beyond your Hope of a Resumption. I need not tell you what Indulgences a Heart susceptible of Love like mine might notwithstanding have allow'd a reasonable or a grateful Woman, nor have I, on the other side, appear'd so mean in my Addresses to you, that you could ever think a Smile could soften me to forget an undeserv'd substantial Wrong, there being as yet but one Action of my Life that I can justly say I am asham'd of, and that* ——*is my late dishonest seeming to ex*cuse *your Injuries, when they were inly* gnawing at my Heart, *and giving me the Rack of an intollerable suppress'd Resentment. I once lov'd you better than my Life, but your insupportable Ingratitude in time wore out, and sunk*

the

the Patience of my exasperated Passion, and now I have sought this desperate Relief.—— I have married you, content to sacrifice the future Quiet of my Life to make yours effectually miserable. Your only Hope is this, That Time may tire my Revenge, and the Pleasure of seeing you in Pain from Repetition, may, like other Pleasures, become insipid to me; then possibly, if you sollicit it, I may consent to a Divorce, which my having never enter'd your Bed will give you an unquestion'd Right to sue for.——For, because I scorn to tast the sensual Happiness of your Beauty, a separate Apartment this Night, and for ever shall divide us——When you are dispos'd there lies your Bed-Chamber——The Company are parted; I prevail'd with my Lord, upon our retiring, to excuse us the usual Impertinencies on these Occasions. To Morrow, at six, the Coach will be ready to carry you into the Country, which I know you hate, but Custom may make it easie to you——

And

And then I intend to bring you up to Town again— 'Tis late — *I'm your Servant.*

Having ended his Oration, he mov'd towards the Door, which not readily unlocking, gave the Lady time to say; *I suppose Sir* Robert, *you don't expect I shou'd make you a Reply; or if I were inclin'd to it, perhaps you think it of no consequence to hear me. Indeed Madam,* (said he) *I don't think it can signifie much at this time; but to let you see I am not out of Temper, and that I have thought before I spoke, I am willing to give you the Hearing.* At this the unblushing Bride, with Spirit in her Eyes, proceeded: *Then, Sir, I own I am not much surpriz'd or disappointed at your Treatment, since all you have said, my Heart can witness, is but the parallel Scheme to what my injur'd Inclination had reserv'd for you; which by your mercenary Interest in my Uncle you have insidiously reduc'd to a constrain'd Surrender of my Person, a Vio-*

Violence more unpardonable, and exceeding far the worst Ingratitude you can reproach me with: How cou'd you then suppose I cou'd remember it without a proportionable Resentment? You think to break my Spirit with the Authority you have gain'd: Go on in your Opinion. As to the Divorce you mention, that will perhaps as much depend on my being weary of Revenge, as yours: In the mean time it can be no great Mortification to have my Bed refus'd by one who never yet cou'd boast he had the least-distant Proof of my Inclination; not but when I consider you as a long neglected Lover, I admire your Spirit in bearing to refrain what once your sighing Heart was bursting to possess; nor can I think that Woman's Beauty is of common Power, that can so distract a Man to undergo such Violence on his Wishes; and since you have paid so dear a Price as Marrying me for your Revenge, what Pangs, what Racks of Heart may I not suppose you have felt? What peircing

The Invisible Witness. 65

peircing Torments must my Neglect have given to provoke you to it ? If after what I have said, one manly Action of your Life convinces me that you as much despise the Offer of my Kindness as my Hate, then I'll confess you Conqueror, and my Pride subdu'd by a superior Spirit; till then at least, I think we are upon equal Terms of Happiness.

 Here the Lady courtesy'd very low, he bow'd; and both putting on a well-bred Smile of Contempt, they retir'd to their separate Apartments. Having thus regal'd my Curiosity, I left them to such Rest as People in so new a Scheme of Happiness may be suppos'd to take.

 And now, ingenious Reader, tho' I am not very much in pain that any Part of this History shou'd be thought fabulous; yet I can't resist giving you my solemn Word, that every Circumstance relating to the Wedding Night is literally true, the rest I am not concern'd to justify; my End in this Work
    I   being

being always answer'd while I am thought instructive or diverting. What you have read is only offer'd as a Specimen of what I farther propose, if the publick Reception of this Part shou'd flatter me to continue the Undertaking.

In the mean time, all Persons that are willing to assist or encourage me, and are curious to know the Truth of Things in doubt; that wou'd be satisfied of the intrinsick Honesty, Virtue, Vice or Follies of Persons in either suspected, or are desirous by an impartial Scrutiny to right (in any Facts) the injur'd Reputation of the Innocent: If any restless Lovers wou'd be reliev'd by a Conviction of their Jealousy: If any inclining Virgins, Wives, Coquets or Prudes, wou'd know what their Admirers, Husbands or other People really think, say or judge of 'em behind their Backs, provided (and at their Peril be it) that no private Pique or Malice prompts them

them to the said Inquiries, let the said Persons inclose a Line to Mr. *Telltale* at Mrs. *Baldwin*'s in *Warwick Lane*, Post-free, and they shall punctually hear in my next whatever in my respective *Invisible Visits* may have pass'd worth their Knowledge, or my Observation.

But it will not be amiss to advise my Correspondents to save themselves the Trouble of giving me any Notice of Persons of extreme Infamy, my Intention being chiefly to confine my Discoveries to the private Faults and Imperfections of such, whose Honour, Rank, Figure or Education, may have made them more modishly capable of disguising them; among which Sort of People, I shall faithfully offer to the Publick whatever appears in my Judgment, Right, Wrong, New, Pleasant or Useful.

FINIS.

Entertainments of Gallantry
Anonymous

Bibliographical note:

This facsimile has been made from a copy in the Beinecke Library of Yale University (College Pamphlets 907)

Entertainments

OF

GALLANTRY:

OR

Remedies for Love.

Familiarly Discours'd, by a Society of Persons of Quality.

———*Amor est medicabilis*——— Ovid.

Ipse quidem nostro Jussu de Corde perusto
Ipse Tyrannorum maximus exit Amor;
Falsus Amor; neq; enim tentas expellere verum.
                      Cowl. Plant. lib. 1st.

LONDON, Read.
Printed for *John Morphew,* near *Stationers-Hall,* 1712.

TO

The GALLANTS of the *British* Nation; *OVID*, from the *Elysiam Fields* sends Greeting.

IT *is with the utmost awe that I approach the Throne of* Beauty, *where so many generous Youths have gloriously languish'd; and after the many fatal Pleasures I essay'd at*
Rome,

Dedication.

Rome, had slept in a quiet and happy Security, had I not been powerfully invok'd by a Witty Assembly, *who was generously willing to give my* Medicinal Thoughts on Love, *a more modern turn, and by calculating 'em more immediately for the present Taste, contribute to the* Advantage *of the* British Youth.

Ah! Ladies, *had you known with what* Anxieties *I past the sometimes tedious, sometimes fleeting Hours, when* Love *usurp'd my Heart, you would never blame the Eagerness I manifest for the better Security*

of

Dedication.

of my Fellow-sufferers, and the Willingness with which I relieve the Youths of Great Britain, *since the Danger is rather greater here,* Beauty's Charms *more powerful, and Youth more Amorous and Yielding.*

But I perceive the Ladies *impatient of my Advice, nor can give the least attention to what endeavours to dispute their Title, and absolute Authority; I hear my self condemn'd as one now insensible of the Pleasures of* Love, *fit only for the airy Conversation of the* Dead, *not Conservation of the* Living.

Dedication.

To foil the Ladies *then at their own Weapons, and allow no excuse for neglecting this Offering of once amorous* Ovid: *Even these* Remedies *for* Love *may be to their Advantage, would they but (conscious of their own Merit) scorn Conquests unworthy of their Charms, for where is the Glory in conquering where there is no manner of Resistance? No, they shall arm their* Lovers *with all my Precautions, shall make 'em worthy their Opposition, and by such Conquests add fresh Lustre to their Beauty. They shall in a word admit no Lover, unless forewarn'd*

Dedication.

warn'd with these Anti-Cupidineal Preparations.

As for the Gallants *of my own Sex, whose Safety I have more particularly regarded; they shall be ever sollicitous, ever careful to defend themselves from the* Inroads *of the little* Urchin, *and the powerful* Charms *of his* Vice-gerent Beauty; *they shall by my* Means *and* Remedies *dispute her Title; endeavour to baffle her cruel* Arts *and ensnaring* Pleasures; *and tho' by Experience I know they must at last quit the Field, for what Mortal can always resist? Yet I*

A 4 *would*

Dedication.

would have 'em sensible, that their Opposition rather proves an Addition to, than Diminution from the Charms of their lovely Fair One, since it renders her more absolute and triumphant.

Oh the happy Emulation that must consequently arise from these Maxims! The Fair Sex will be only ambitious of conquering where they are oppos'd; and the generous Youths will by my Assistance indulge their Charmer's Ambition, heighten her Power by the Opposition they make, and show the World that the Charms that conquer'd them

Dedication.

them were irresistably Victorious.

It had been wholly inexcusable in me, though wrapt in Shades of Night, *to have deny'd my* Approbation *to a* Work *so consistent with my* Design, *and advantageous to the* Beau-monde ; *nor should I have thought my* Honour *in the least diminish'd, had the same* witty, agreeable Assembly, *detain d me for the entire Revolution of a* Moon, *while they were giving my* Art of Loving *the same beautiful Additions : But I am more than satisfy'd, in finding my* Name *admir'd among the*

Dedication.

the Ladies, *and my* Works *instrumental to their* Diversion; *'tis herein I re-enjoy the past* Pleasures *of* Rome, *and in the height of my* Satisfaction *conclude my self,*

Ladies and Gentlemen,

Your

Amorous Physician,

Publius Ovidius Naso.

THE

THE
PREFACE.

SINCE it is a Truth so universally held as admits of no doubt that the Excellence of a Remedy ought to be judg'd of, according to the Nature and Fierceness of the Disease it prevails over: It must consequently be allow'd that nothing has, or ever can be committed to publick View; whose intrinsick Value may be comparable to this small Treatise, since it proposes a Remedy for Love, the greatest and most universal Malady now reigning. What Age, Sex or Condition has been able to defend it self from its Inroads? Examples of all Kinds are too frequent and obvious, without having recourse beyond this our Metropolis? I could cite a profest *Devotée*, who would bless herself at the least soft or passionate Expression utter'd

The Preface.

ter'd in her Presence; a meer walking Skeleton, furrow'd with Wrinkles; and in a word, a firm Maintainer of this rigid piece of Morals, talk'd of universally, but an utter Stranger to Practice: Yet is not she at last an humble passionate Votary at *Cupid*'s Shrine, in love with a Divine, young, fair and handsome; to him she has sacrific'd her *Heart*, *Bed* and *Estate*, to the no small Confusion of her proper Heirs.

A Second carries her Precautions to a larger Extent, even to forcing an only *Daughter* to the same Bed, with an *Old Maiden Aunt*; and herself by Night, and to a constant Confinement in her inner Chamber all Day: Yet *Love* finds Methods of deceiving these watchful *Argus*'s; and procures a settled Commerce between the two Lovers.

A certain *Knight*, who has all good Qualities united, and in the greatest Perfection; who is without Vanity, of high *Birth*, gentile *Carriage*, *Valiant*, *Witty* and *Agreeable*; now loves and is belov'd by

The Preface.

by a *young Lady* of incomparable Beauty. Powerful Love forces him from the Purſuit of Glory, lends him his Wings to fly into her Arms, where inſtead of the raviſhing Pleaſures he expected to enjoy, the *treacherous Deity* ſees him expiring at her Feet.

Nor is the *Church* Proof againſt the *Encroachments* of this lovely Seducer. Have we not ſeen the moſt *Devout* corrupted by this Paſſion, even in their moſt ſecret *Receſſes*; and hurry'd by the Violence of its Attractions to *Places*, conſecrated in a peculiar manner to *Love* and *Pleaſure*.

Was it permitted to ſearch the *Sanctuaries* of *Princes*, we ſhould find him there. Theſe *Monarchs* of the *World* languiſh in the ſame Torment, under this *Tyrant's Yoak*; and oftentimes the violent Motions, that even ſhake the Univerſe; the Deluges of Blood daily ſpilt, and attributed to the ambitious Deſire of enlarging Kingdoms; are in effect no more than Love-tricks, and Secret in-

The Preface.

intreagues of an imperious Beauty, who takes a haughty Pleasure in seeing a *Triumphant Victor* prostrate at her Feet.

There would be no end of recounting all the Evils, Love is the fatal Cause of; *Pandora*'s Box is but an *Epitome* of the Plagues *Cupid* daily torments Mankind with. He is to the Heart, if we will credit a *modern Wit*, what a Fever is to the Body; and since the shiverings in an Ague, are not so violent as those of an impotent and jealous old *Cuff*; continually dreading the Danger, a Troop of handsome young Fellows, laying close Siege to his Wife, expose his Imaginary Honour to: His hot Fits being terrible, and not be equall'd; their Venom immediately seizes the Heart, thence communicating it self to the Brain in violent Transports, leaves him destitute of both *Sense* and *Reason*.

A Girl once thus infected, utterly rejects her *Virgin Modesty* and *Decency*: A Wife her Promises, and solemn Engagements of the *Marriage-Vow*: Soldiers

The Preface.

diers their *Fortune* and *Ambition*: The Magistrate his *Justice*, and due observance of the Laws: And the Prince his *Grandeur* and *Majesty*.

Some indeed have been of Opinion, that Absence would prove an Antidote to this prevaling Passion: But let 'em remember the wretched *Dido*; *Æneas*'s Flight was so far from effecting her Cure, that it was the real Cause of her unfortunate Exit.

If then it must be indisputably agreed, that those Distempers are most dangerous, wherein the *Heart* and *Brain* share the Infection; and that this is the sure Effect, and cruel Symptom of Love: It must consequently be allow'd by all Mankind, that too great a Value, can never be set upon a Book; which contains a Remedy for so raging a Distemper. And, what ought yet more to enhance your Esteem, the Remedy, contrary to common Practice is gentle, agreeable, and to be purchas'd at an Expence, not worth naming.

THE

THE CONTENTS.

THE First Entertainment, p. 1.
The pleasant Adventure of Timante, p. 4.
The Second Entertainment, p. 21.
The Third Entertainment, p. 31.
The History of Clidamas, and young Doris, p. 38.
The Fourth Entertainment, p. 44.
The Comical History of Damon, Jealous of his own Shadow, p. 55.
The Fifth Entertainment, p. 61.
The Sixth Entertainment, p. 71.
The History of Fidelio and Lysander, p. 79.

SIX ENTERTAINMENTS OF GALLANTRY:

OR Remedies for LOVE.

The First ENTERTAINMENT.

THE length and real tediousness of the Winter Season makes every one impatient for its End, that they may breath a more refin'd Air, free from the choaking Fogs of this Town, and eas'd of the Burthen of Business. The succeeding Spring seems but half agreeable, by the Interposition of some fine Weather, that restores the Fields their delightful Verdure. In the Summer we are swelter'd with Heat, or choak'd with Dust, and can find but small Intervals of time for enjoying the fresh Air. But Autumn is in my Opinion the most charming Season of the Year. The Heat's allay'd allay'd by cool refreshing Breezes, and the Fruits of the Earth seem to invite us to a delightful and magnificent Collation. Nor is it in vain; we are eager to enjoy the grateful Returns benign Nature makes. The Town becomes a Solitude. Business, Trades, nay what was once thought Pleasure, is now willingly quitted for the more engaging, and more innocent Delights of the Country, which now abounds with great Variety of good Company: The *Bath*, *Tunbridge*, *Richmond*, *Epsom*, are now the only Scenes of Pleasure. The Court-end of the Town, where the *Beau-monde* usually resorts, at this time appearing dull and melancholy, I was resolv'd among the rest to share the inviting Pleasures of the Country; and with this Design, went to pass some Days at *Epsom*, which the Goodness of the Air, and Mineral Waters have made Famous. I follow'd the old Custom, and drank 'em every Morning, less medicinally, than for the Pleasure of a Walk. The Company was numerous, and every Morning most agreeably lost, in the variety of Persons, pleasant in Humour and Conversation. We constituted at last a select Society of Six or Seven, whose Company seem'd most grateful to each other; and enter'd into variety of agreeable Conversation. Those, who to heighten the Pleasures of Retreat, had brought Books with 'em, communicated 'em to the Company; and this afforded variety of Discourse on very entertaining Subjects. As we had some Ladies, excelling both in Wit and Beauty, the Stream of Discourse was immediately turn'd to Gallantry and Love.

One

One remark'd, that the Gallants of our Island were less sensible of the Power of Love, than that of the Bottle, and often suffer'd Strangers to usurp their Priviledges with the Ladies.

A second mov'd a word or two, touching *Ovid*'s Amours, and took a small Treatise out of her Pocket: I reach'd it out of her Hand, and opening it, found it was his *Remedium Amoris*. All the Company laugh'd at this pleasant Mistake; and agreed this Book should serve us all the Week, with the principal Subjects of our Discourse.

In walking we happen'd to light accidentally upon a Place cover'd with a shady Green, and equally endebted to Art and Nature for its Embellishments. Oh! The charming Place, cry'd a Gentleman, full of Admiration, how convenient? How proper for Love and the Muses?

True, interrupted a Lady, but in my Opinion, much more convenient for the Muses than Love: The little Deity is best engag'd in the Concourse of Company; nor has the Country those Charms for him, it once could boast of; Solitude is tedious, and he is easier lull'd to sleep by Consorts of Musick, than the Murmurings of a purling Stream.

This Place being appointed for our present assembling, some one propos'd the reading Precepts of Gallantry in Verse; but was answer'd, that this Age had little or no relish for Verses; that the World was quite fatigu'd with the ridiculous Works of *Wou'd-be-Poets*; and that Poesie was never so near its end as now; it is an Art very few can succeed in, and I join with him that said *Verses, like Melons, if not perfectly good, are worth nothing*; let's return then to our first Design. Immediately he began.

B 2 It

It is an approv'd Maxim among several Ladies, that now-a-days Men are rarely afflicted in Love, and even at its height, don't stand in need of great Remedies to cure 'em of their Passion; that Inconstancy, Caprice, and Distaste are their ordinary Medicines. But would they be more just to themselves, they'd find this Opinion no less satyrical on the Ladies than the Men: They ought to have a better Opinion of their own Power; a wound from a piercing Eye is not so easily cur'd, there is need of Soveraign Remedies to ensure a Recovery. They'll object perhaps, that what I say argues more of Gallantry than Truth, and so endeavour to persuade themselves that this Age can boast of very few true Lovers. But should they seem so certain of our Inconstancy, I shall be apt to believe they speak by too fatal Experience. However, I still maintain the Female Sex to be full as fickle as ours; and that if we prove Inconstant 'tis very often after their Example. I could cite a thousand Proofs in this Matter, but I'll content my self with an Adventure an intimate Friend of mine was very lately engag'd in; and concealing his Name, give you his History under the borrow'd Name of *Timante*.

The pleasant Adventure of TIMANTE.

Timante is a young Gentleman, Genteel and Gallant; his Wit answers his good Mien; and what's yet more necessary to the compleating a Lover, he is one that loves violently and faithfully at the same time. *Felicia*, for so we'll call his false Mistress, was the first Charmer of his

Heart,

Heart, nor was it his Fault that she lost a Power she might have maintain'd 'till Death. He plac'd his entire Satisfaction in pleasing her, nor did he ever displease. *Felicia* testify'd the like ardent Passion for him, and they tasted all the Pleasures Love could bestow on two united Hearts. But this Calm was too sweet to last. *Timante* was oblig'd to absent himself on some important Business; and no doubt their Adieus were as tender as fatal; *Timante* I'm apt to believe wept, and *Felicia* in that Point out-did him; for with Submission, Ladies, you have a much better Talent that way than we can pretend to, the Gift of Tears really belonging to your Sex. *Timante* ever faithful, gave her all Assurances an absent Lover can give a Person he adores; I would intimate by this, that he writ the most passionate Letters imaginable. She did not fail on her side to assure him, that Absence should rather heighten her Passion, and he might be satisfied of finding her at his return as passionate as ever. She promis'd indeed, but without design of Performance. She was tir'd with sighing so long for an absent Lover, and entertain'd a fatal Opinion, that she might languish in a new Passion, without unhappy *Timante*'s Knowledge, and that at last so long an Absence would surely justify a small Infidelity. A young Spark her Neighbour, whom I'll call *Lycidas*, was continually solliciting her, and endeavouring to confirm her in her new founded Maxim; wherein he at last succeeded. In a word, he supplanted, by his frequent Visits the too faithful, and too wretched *Timante*, who no ways advis'd of *Felicia*'s Infidelity, continu'd his Letters equally passionate for one whose sole endeavour

deavour was to play the Traytor. She, to take away all Suspicion of her Inconstancy, still answer'd him with the same Care and Passion as before; and had the Inhumanity to deceive the faithfullest Lover on Earth. But Love will never suffer such perfidy to go unpunish'd. *Timante* having happily accomplish'd his Business sooner than his Mistress expected, resolv'd to have the Satisfaction of surprizing her. He began his Journey without giving her any Notice, and the Moment he came to Town went to her House. By Misfortune *Felicia* had that Day appointed a Rendezvous, with her new Lover, they were both together, and when they least expected *Timante*, heard his Voice below Stairs. I leave you to judge their Surprize; *Felicia* immediately hid *Lycidas* in a Closet, and all astonish'd ran to intercept *Timante*. She rally'd her utmost Dissimulation to her Assistance, and embrac'd him with so extravagant an Extasie, that a Lover less prepossess'd in his Mistress's Favour, might have easily been deceiv'd. But it was not possible to be so much Mistress of her self, as to hide so visible a Confusion from his Eyes. *Timante* perceiv'd it, and thence presag'd no good to his Love; but was more confirm'd in his Suspicions, when having desir'd her Company some part of the Night, that he might enjoy a Conversation he had so long been depriv'd of, she cunningly endeavour'd to divert his Intentions; she alledg'd a thousand Reasons, which were so far from answering the desir'd Effect, that they rather made him more earnest in his Demands. She durst not however absolutely deny it, and being apprehensive of his suspecting the whole Truth, endeavour'd to divert him
other-

otherways. Still Night came on; *Felicia* was strangely discompos'd, she was willing to free *Lycidas* from his Prison, but saw no likelihood of his Deliverance. Fortune seem'd to favour her in this Quandary. Her Father was that Day gone in the Country, and not returning, her Mother, like most Women of her Age, having strange dreadful Apprehensions of Spirits, would not lie alone, but sent for her Daughter to share her Bed. *Felicia* transported at this Pretext, soon acquainted her Lover with her Mother's Orders, which he seem'd inclinable to believe, the better to ensnare her by this feign'd Confidence. He still imagin'd some design on Foot, and was really persuaded in his Mind, that she intended nothing more than to deceive him. He dissembled his Thoughts, and promis'd her he would immediately go out by a back pair of Stairs he was acquainted with. She believing him, left him in her Chamber, and went to her Mother's Bed; but in her way could not forbear visiting *Lycidas* out of Charity; who was storming at *Timante*, as interrupter of his Happiness. She comforted him, acquainted him how luckily she got clear, and promis'd him to slip out of Bed from her Mother, and pass an hour or two with him in the Closet. She immediately went to Bed, but took this necessary Precaution not to lock her Chamber Door, lest the Noise she must unavoidably make at her going out should wake her Mother. She waited impatiently for the good Woman's sleeping, and to encourage it seem'd to sleep her self. *Timante* all this while had little reason to be satisfied: Far from going out as he promis'd her, he began now to reflect on the Confusion *Feli-*

cia was in at his Appearance, her Reasons good or bad for his absenting himself; and above all a certain hurry and perplexity that appear'd in all her Words and Actions. These Reflections plung'd him into a deep Concern; He thought . . . . more than I can express; he thought all a jealous Lover could think at such a Juncture. Willing to be better inform'd, he repair'd to the Mother's Chamber to see if *Felicia* was really there or no: He found the Door half open, bad Presage! He went softly to the Bed-side, and felt two Persons, whom he suppos'd the Mother and Daughter. *Felicia*, who all this while slept Dog-sleep, soon perceiv'd her jealous Lover, instead of going away, was resolv'd to sound the Bottom, and accordingly came as a Spy. *Timante* by this a little better satisfied, was going away, when coming nearer the Door he heard something stir; 'twas indeed *Lycidas*, who like a true Lover, tir'd with Expectation, and fearing she might be really fallen asleep, was coming in Person to wake her. Hearing a Noise, and conjecturing 'twas his fair one that advanc'd towards him, whisper'd in a gentle Voice, *you've stay'd an Age my Dear.* *Timante* with his usual Presence of Mind, counterfeiting her Voice, answer'd, *I was just now coming, walk forward, and I'll follow.* *Lycidas* went on full of Love and Hope with *Timante* at his Heels: But how great was his Surprize when he found by the Light of the Flambeaux his Mistake, and saw instead of his expected Mistress a dangerous Rival? Jealousie had then an absolute sway in *Timante*'s Heart, and he was at the very point of sacrificing *Lycidas* to his Resentment, when *Felicia* enter'd the Closet. Tho' they had made little Noise during

during this fatal Interview, it was sufficient to alarm her. She presently conjectur'd *Lycidas*'s Error, and had dreadful Apprehensions what the Effects of it might prove. She ran to the Closet, *Go unfaithful*. *Timante* began at her Entry, *Go base perfidious Woman, you have here been guilty of the blackest Ingratitude in Nature. Did I think my Love injur'd, I would this moment sacrifice you both to attone for your joint Sin, or meet my fate from his Sword; but you are not worthy my least Anger, and I'll henceforward look upon you with more horror than the worst of Creatures.* In finishing these Words, he left 'em abruptly, and made his way down the back Stairs into the Street, but the Confusion they remain'd in is inexpressible.

The reciting this Adventure in Company made every one willing to moralize, and give his Opinion on the Matter.

For God's sake, says a Lady, give me no more Histories of this sort; Men afford no less ample matter of Discourse on this Subject, than the Ladies; tho' with this Advantage over us, that they're allow'd publickly to discant on their Mistresses Infidelity, a Liberty our Modesty utterly debars us from. I believe your Friend was deceiv'd; but give me leave to imagine, at the same time, whatever you may alledge in his Favour, that he has deceiv'd some Innocent in his turn, who was oblig'd to be silent. Neither is his Misfortune so deplorable, for by what I can understand, he was soon comforted for *Felicia*'s Inconstancy. I pity indeed a Lover, who tho' deceiv'd by an inconstant Mistress, has not the Power to quit her Chains; and rather encreases his Passion, by Proofs of her Infidelity. Such a Lover deserves a Remedy, and I heartily wish

the

the Author of the Precepts of Gallantry would make *Ovid*'s Remedies of Love agree with this Opinion.

(*Ovid*, the moſt experienc'd Maſter, having paſs'd through all the Gallantries of the *Roman* Court; gives us Precepts for the preventing this diſorderly Paſſion, by ſtifling it at its Birth. For when once the Heart's become ſubject, it is no longer poſſible to reſiſt the univerſal Conqueror even of all Mankind. Diligence in this Caſe is ſo abſolutely neceſſary, that Delays make it but more dangerouſly ſtubborn and difficult to maſter. The Seducer flatters us into an Amuſement, and in our Irreſolution ruins us. We muſt never pretend to vye cunning with him, the Moment we begin to dally, he gains a Conqueſt.)

Tho' *Ovid* ſpeaks very juſtly, ſome one might alledge, that the Empire of Love would no longer be abſolute, but ſoon become unpeopled, was the World faithfully to obſerve this Precept. His Arrors would be uſeleſs, his Torch extinguiſh'd, and we ſhould ſpare our ſelves a thouſand Inquietudes which now inevitably attend us. But alaſs! we are ſeldom capable of making a right Uſe of wholeſome Remedies. We perſuade our ſelves we have no occaſion, are moſt ingenious to our own Deceit, and oftentimes dangerouſly ill, yet ignorant of our Caſe, or at leaſt unwilling to undeceive our ſelves. Love inſinuates himſelf inſenſibly, that he may without alarming the Heart to a Defence, gain Admittance: Sports, Pleaſures, and all that can be call'd ſoft and agreeable are his Forerunners; and the Heart greedily entertains 'em; gives up it ſelf entirely to its violent Tranſports, and

Experience makes evident, that it is less difficult not to Love at all, than to Love with Moderation.

You speak with a great deal of reason, Madam, reply'd a Gentleman, it is the real Character of most Tempers. We find it difficult to retain either in our Humours or Actions, a certain Medium, tho' so absolutely necessary both to the one and the other. A liberal Soul has the greatest Difficulty in the World, to set Bounds to his Expences: Good Husbandry often degenerates into Covetousness; and Courage is very often sullied with the extreme of Rashness: But this is more allowable in Love. A Lover is of Opinion he wrongs his Mistress, if he does not manifest an excess of Love; he persuades himself her Charms would be injur'd by a Passion less than violent, and that to shew the World how amiable she appears in his Eyes, he ought to Love even to Desperation. This argues *Ovid*'s Precept perfectly just, but at the same time as perfectly useless. When Love first aims at a Mastery over the Heart, we neglect making a Defence; and when once he becomes absolute, we may undertake a cure, but our endeavours will prove vain. *Ovid* however supposes a Possibility, and expresses himself to this Effect.

(At Love's first Birth, endeavour to expel the Poison, but if once he becomes Victor at the Expence of your Reason, proceed cautiously, your hasty Endeavours, will but encrease the Flame, which once grown calm is easily o'ercome.)

This is expresly, reply'd a Lady, the Maxim we handled before; that Love is not to be expell'd, pell'd, when he once grows violent. Is it not apparent that *Ovid* is of this Opinion; and advises a Toleration 'till the firſt Storms are over? He preſcribes no Remedy 'till the Diminution of the Evil, and all his Counſel tends to no other Effect, than the extirpating the Remains of a Paſſion, which would ſoon dye of it ſelf. We ſhould really have great Obligations to his Art, did he work a Cure, when the Diſeaſe is in its greateſt Vigour; did he undeceive his Votaries, recal their ſtraggling Reaſon, and re-eſtabliſh 'em in the State, he would willingly ſee 'em, before his undertaking their Cure: This would indeed prove a Maſter-piece. But far from attempting this bold Stroke, he leaves 'em entirely at the Conqueror's Mercy: He is reduc'd to make Vows in favour of his Suppliants; and they have a thouſand Opportunities of expiring before he comes to their Aid.

However we won't lay all the fault on *Ovid*, let's give him his due. All endeavours ought to be us'd in this Affair, but the Violence of a Diſeaſe will ſometimes baffle our Art; and there is no Force or Obligation to cure Wounds incurable. It is ſufficient he can preſcribe Remedies to ſtrengthen us in a languiſhing Condition, and prevent a relapſe, always dangerous and often Mortal. But if you pleaſe Sir, continu'd the Lady, let's hear the Sequel of his Precepts: The Gentleman immediately took up the Diſcourſe and ſaid,

(Shun Idleneſs, for then his Arrows are doubly mortal; they are inſeparable Companions, and Love is often call'd *the Child of Idleneſs*. When one has nothing to do, what can one do but Love?)

Ah!

Ah! Sir, reply'd a young Lady, smiling, tho' I were sure you'd take it ill, I could not avoid interrupting your Carreer. Oh! how charming the Expression? How ravishing the Thought? I can scarce contain my self. Let me beg of you Sir, to give me a Copy of this excellent Precept, for a Prude of my Acquaintance; I shall infinitely oblige her in it, and I don't question but she'll have it engrav'd in Letters of Gold in every Corner of her Chamber.

It is impossible, Madam, answer'd he, I should take an Interruption ill that afforded such an agreeable Entertainment; on the contrary I shall desire it oftner, that so I may oftner have the Pleasure of hearing you speak: He continu'd, and said,

(Idleness nourishes the Flames of Love, and Occupation alone can extinguish 'em. *Pallas* and *Bellona* have so many and so useful Employments, that it is an absolute shame to be Idle.)

There's a charming Precept, says a Gentleman, and not a little advantageous for those that can come up to its Doctrine. *Ovid* himself, tho' our Author, had not the Power to put it in Practice. We no where read of his ever making use of this Remedy, tho' without doubt he has not wanted occasions, having shewn himself a general Adorer of all the Ladies at *Rome*. If the great *Augustus* had no better Soldiers than *Ovid*, I doubt, he would never have given Laws to the whole Universe. The Poet was better qualified to force his Mistress's Chamber-door, than the Enemies Lines, and could scale a Window much easier than the Walls of a Town. I believe he was apprehensive of some Reproach this way, and so advanc'd a Justification in one of his Love-Elegies,

Elegies, address'd to his Friend *Atticus*. He endeavours there to prove with good Reasons, that Love is a kind of War; that *Cupid* boasts of his pitch'd Fields, Camps and Battles, equally with *Mars*, and equally of the Fatigues; that Courage and Conduct are no less useful in the Chamber than in the Field; and in a Word, that the Glory is as great in triumphing over our Charmer's Heart, as in gaining a Battle. But this Subject will demand the utmost force of his Rhetorick, to persuade the World of their pretended Equality; and all his admirable reasoning only manifests, his great Inclinations for Peace, and that he could much better agree in shedding Tears, than Blood. Certainly ———

Hold, Sir, shew some Mercy to the poor Gentleman, says a Lady interrupting him, far from ridiculing his peaceable Inclination as you do, (tho' perhaps without Reason) you ought to applaud it in him, and return thanks to *Apollo* as to the Donor. How great would have been the Loss to Love, and its Votaries, if that Hand which writ so many and so fine Pieces, had shewn a greater fancy to weild a Sword, than handle a Pen; and by exposing himself to the hazards of a Battle, had lost a Life, so well employ'd since, for the Pleasure and Satisfaction as well as Instruction of all the World? Not that I doubt his Courage; his Birth was too noble to want it; and you'll wonder perhaps when I shall make it appear a principal of Generosity, that hinder'd him from engaging in the Wars. Great Men love no Rivals in Glory: In *Ovid*'s Time Bravery was common; the being born a *Roman* was sufficient for the making a brave Soldier; and few were noted in the Army, whose Courage

rage was not push'd to the utmost Extremity. *Ovid* rather approv'd the Honour of being excellent in an Art he profest, than to be confounded in the Croud of brave Commanders of his Age.

Perhaps, added another Lady, he was willing to observe the Edict formerly made by the *Greeks*, who by Misfortune, having had one of their Poets slain in Battle; prohibited all of that Profession, the taking up Arms for the future.

Oh! the happy Edict, cry'd another Lady, and how devoutly observ'd by the Poets of our Age.

You are continually saying some pretty Witticism, Madam, reply'd a Gentleman, but really, you don't deal justly by these Men of Parts. There was found among the *Greeks* and *Romans*, Men that equally signaliz'd themselves in Arms and Wit, and in the same Hand that lately writ some lofty Ode, or melting Elegy, held a Sword reeking with the Blood of the Enemies of their Country. Nor are there wanting even in our time Persons who have join'd Bravery to Learning; and to speak Poetically, when alluding to Poets, have been equally Favorites of *Mars*, and *Minerva*. Indeed, continu'd she, there are some great Scholars that seldom or never take up Arms; but that ought to be imputed to the weakness of their Constitutions, (Study being not a little destructive to the *Health*) rather than to default of Courage; they rather chuse to give a great Action its due Praises, than to be real Actors in it.

If then, reply'd a Countess smiling, these Persons should be in Love; *Ovid*'s Prescription of War, for the extirpating their Passion, would

be

be altogether uſeleſs to them; they'd find the Exerciſe too violent.

There are others then, reply'd a Gentleman, not ſo harſh, and yet will have the ſame Effect; you'll perceive it by the following one.

(Should the War prove too harſh, repair to the Woods, run down a Hare, Stag or wild Boar, and you'll perceive when you return home at Night, fatigu'd with the troubles of the Day, more inclination to ſleep than to make Love.)

Ovid's really in the right, ſays Sir W—— for when one is tir'd, Sleep is more proper to be indulg'd, than a Paſſion for a Miſtreſs, and ſhe perhaps cruel. Beſides it is evident our Hearts can't ſuffer two different Inclinations at once: It ſeems as if one deſtroy'd the other, and he that gives himſelf up entirely to Hunting, has little room for Love. The E—l of S—— is a moſt extraordinary Example of this kind: You are all ſenſible that he was one of the greateſt Gallants at Court; never was Man more admir'd by the Ladies, nor was their Admiration ever better requited. I can't imagine what diſguſt he took of a ſudden, there are a thouſand different Sentiments of it; but his Mind was at once wholly taken up with Hunting. Before he frequented the Woods for the ſolitary Indulging his amorous Thoughts; now, ſtrange Metamorphoſis! he is never ſeen there, but 'midſt a confus'd noiſe of Horns, running down a timorous Hare or Stag. His Dogs have uſurp'd the Heart, his Miſtreſſes once triumph'd over, and he now ſhows as much Indifference for all the fair Sex, as before he did Inclination and Reſpect.

So Sir, reply'd a Gentleman, ſo much for Examples that prove nothing. Take my Word,

Love

Love is the ſtrongeſt, or rather the only Paſſion; the World indeed falſely attributes Hunting, Gaming, Study, and whatever we manifeſt the leaſt Inclination for, to Paſſions; but if they'd but give themſelves the liberty to look to the bottom, they'd be convinc'd how unjuſtly that Title's given 'em; for ſpeaking properly Love is the only Paſſion of the Heart: There is nothing can come in Competition with it, much leſs eradicate it. The Empire of other Amuſements is ſhort; they have not always Entertainment, neither Play nor Study; but what Time is there, wherein we can't Love? *Cephalus* may abſent himſelf, even in the deep Receſs of a Foreſt, and make the Woods eccho with the Cries of his Hounds; but Love regards not the Noiſe he purſues, and the charming *Aurora* is ever before his Eyes. In vain *Hyppolitus* leaves his Palace, and abandons himſelf to a ſolatary Life in the inhoſpitable Woods; in vain he implores *Diana*'s Aid againſt Love; *Aricia* never leaves him; ſhe is always preſent to his afflicted Mind. His Caſe is admirably expreſs'd by an excellent *French* Author, in a Tragedy of that Name, which runs thus.

For ſix long Moons full of Deſpair and Shame,
Hugging the Dart which cauſes all my Pain;
'Gainſt you, againſt myſelf, I try my Mind, [*I find.*
Your Charms when preſent do attract, abſent their force
You're preſent where thick Trees obſcure the Light,
The Sun's no remedy, nor Shades of Night;
The Charms I ſhun are with me ev'ry where,
Rebel Hyppolitus *is all Deſpair:*
Vain Fruit of all my Cares I now look round,
To ſeek a ſelf, is no where to be found:
My Bow, and Arrows lie, ignobly on the Ground.

C Great

Great Neptune's *Precepts I forget*⸺
The Woods resound, with my Groans hollow Noise,
And my own Coursers have forgot my Voice.

You see Sir, continu'd he, the Confession *Hyppolitus* makes to his charming *Aricia*. The Author that introduces him in this manner, is better acquainted than I perceive you are with the Nature and Power of Love. He was sensible nothing on Earth was able to secure it self from *Cupid*'s Force, and that endeavouring to flie the Charmer's Presence, we can never flie from our selves, where the Danger lies. All manner of Amusement is vain and useless, nor can ever disengage a Heart from the Object Love has inspir'd it with. All it can effect is to render it less attentive to the Evil, and so sometimes sooth its Violence.

And do you count that nothing Sir, reply'd a Divine? For my part, I think it not inconsiderably advantageous. And whatever you can alledge, I am of Opinion, that these Amusements, since you are pleas'd to give 'em that Title, produce yet greater Effects. Whatever time we spend therein, is stole from Love. These small Thefts, not a little weaken him; and we have at least this Advantage of convincing our selves of the Possibility of shaking off his Yoak for ever, since we can do it for some time. And whoever can prevail so much over himself, as to employ his Heart otherwise than in Loving, may insensibly perceive the Ardour of his Love decay. Love subsists by continual Practice, and perishes by an opposite Habitude: It has a strong Power over those alone whose Loving is their only Employment.

Ovid

Ovid proposes yet two more very much us'd in his Time, but little regarded now, they are, Agriculture and Fishing. No one can be ignorant, in what esteem the first of these was held by the Ancient *Romans*: 'Twas the ordinary Employment of Gentlemen, who thought it no Disgrace to plant Trees, or cultivate Gardens, and turn the Course of a River for the more commodious watering 'em. We read too of Persons taken from the Plough, to command victorious Armies, and the Conquerours had the Pleasure of seeing themselves crown'd with that Laurel, their own Hand had planted. Fishing was not less familiar, and I am apt to Conjecture, that 'twas to divert themselves from this innocent Exercise, when the great *Scipio*, and his Companion, were found employ'd in gathering Shells on the Sea-side. But since they are no longer practis'd, it would be ridiculous to advise Lovers to such Remedies. I have here another; it is not indeed extream tender, but shall be my last at this time; I'll then resign my Place to any of the Company, that at our next Rendezvous shall have the Courage to enter the Lists.

(If you are willing to overcome a Passion already raging; search for a Remedy by Absence from the Object of your Affections; never think of going back, the Essay is too dangerous. Flight is absolutely necessary; nor ought you to reflect how far you have already gone, but what yet remains to go. In a word, your Absence must be very long, or not at all; a short Absence is to be fear'd: Love makes use of it to gather more Strength; and a Lover after such a short Space finds his fair One really more Aimable, and loves her accordingly more than ever.)

Very well spoken, reply'd the Countess, you could never have ended by a more useful Thought, nor better express'd. This frequently occurs to Lovers; but I can't imagine by what Caprice it happens, that their Love augments by being for a small time depriv'd of the Sight of their Mistresses. Pray whence comes this double Violence of Love? Is it not, that during their Absence they have had the Leisure to think millions of tender things, which being lock'd up in the Chamber of their Hearts for some Days, rush out with Violence at the Sight of their lovely Cause; like a Torrent that encreases and flows with greater Impetuosity when it has surmounted the Banks that oppos'd its Course.

Is it not, added Sir W―――― that *Cupid* disdaining the Efforts a Lover, makes use of to shake off his Tyranny; pleases himself in making him more sensible of his Power, and engages him more strongly in his Chains, to punish him for the Design he had of making his Escape.

For my part I believe, added a young Lady, that a Heart is weaken'd by the Contests a Lover has held against himself, and endeavouring to triumph o're his Passion, he really abandons himself more entirely to it; for not being able to succeed, he is forced to sweat under a Yoke, he has not been able to disengage himself from.

We need not go so far for Reasons, reply'd a Gentleman of the Company, it is evident we seldom give a Blessing we possess the just value. It seems as tho' Possession lessen'd the Esteem, and that we are never satisfied of the Price 'till the Loss is irreparable. A generous Lover sometimes sleeps in his fair one's Company, is careless in his Applications, and knows not the worth of her Charms, because he has the liberty

of

of vifiting her when he pleafes. But let him be at fome confiderable Diftance, then the impoffibility of feeing her, doubles his Defires, and makes him fenfible of fuch amorous Impatiencies, as he was before an utter Stranger to. He burns with defire of her Company, and flies to glut himfelf with a fight of thofe Beauties, he has fo long been depriv'd of. Love anfwers his Ends in thefe Tranfports, and four or five Days Abfence, advances a Love-Affair more, than a whole Month's affiduous Applications.

You fhall have it your own way, interrupted a young Lady, for we have philofophiz'd enough on this Subject, and never confider when to retire.

The Company immediately arofe from their Seats, and the Pleafures of a Walk fucceeded that of fo witty and fo agreeable a Converfation.

The Second ENTERTAINMENT.

THE preceding Days Converfation had fo charm'd the witty Affembly, that it is no wonder, they were fo careful to meet the fucceeding Night, at the fame Hour, that they might enjoy a fecond, which in all Appearance would not afford lefs matter of Entertainment than the firft. The Company had fcarce feated themfelves, paid reciprocal Compliments, and given an account how each had pafs'd the tedious Night; when a Lady firft mov'd the Difcourfe, and faid, fhe had fcarce flept a wink for thinking, and that the Injunctions of the Company had fo diforder'd her, that fhe had feveral times repented her having undertaken fo difficult a Task.

The neceſſity I find my ſelf under, continu'd the Lady, of ſpeaking againſt the Intereſt of my own Sex, together with the ſmall Inſight I have in the Elegancies of the Tongue *Ovid* writ in, made me not a little uneaſy. But by meer good Fortune, among the few Books I always keep in my Cloſet, I found a Tranſlation of *Ovid*'s Art of Loving, and Remedies of Love in Proſe. I read it with a great deal of Application, and endeavour'd as much as poſſible to make my ſelf Miſtreſs of *Ovid*'s Meaning. I began by the Place where we left off Yeſterday: I think it was by counſelling Lovers to long Voyages; and adviſing 'em in Abſence to ſeek a Remedy for the Inhumanity of their Miſtreſſes.

I muſt acknowledge the Remedy excellent, but not general: Buſineſs, Employment, or Dependancies, often engage Men to thoſe Places where the Danger lies. There may be no avoiding a ſight of 'em, and ſometimes even a neceſſity of ſpeaking to 'em. *Ovid* foreſaw this, and in conſideration, inſtructs 'em how they may ſafely live with their Charmers, when there is no poſſibility of avoiding it. He diſcourſes largely on this Point, and not without Reaſon, for a Lover is always in danger of a Relapſe, at the Sight of his charming Miſtreſs, and has need of powerful Remedies for an Evil that threatens him ſo nearly. This is his firſt.

(If you would free your ſelf from the Follies of Love; only call to mind the Torments you have ſuffer'd, thro' the preſent and paſt Rigours of a cruel Miſtreſs. Weigh the time you loſe in her Service, and ſay all a Heart would urge, that was willing to break its Bonds aſunder. Say the Ungrateful ſhe betrays you; that ſhe's unfaithful, and ſhews another Countenance, whoſe

Merit

Merit is not comparable to yours: Refift with Force the magnetick Inftinct, that naturally attracts you to her Charms. Repeat this Remedy, even a hundred times a Day, and you will at laft either arrive to hating, or at leaft to a more fuccefsful Indifference, which will revenge your paft Pains.)

Give me leave, Madam to interrupt you, reply'd the Divine, that I may fufficiently admire the happy turn you give *Ovid*'s Thought; 'tis clear and witty, nor is it poffible to exprefs a lively Senfe in fewer Words: I only wifh it could as eafily be experienc'd, as exprefs'd: But ah! Madam, continu'd he, a Heart perfectly in Love, is not fo eafily made free. In vain does the Charmer fet us an Example of Inconftancy, it is impoffible to imitate it, and our Love rather augments, and grows more fervent by her Inconftancy and Perfidioufnefs.

Add to this, reply'd a Gentleman, that her Change makes us yet more eager for Poffeffion; we are all on fire to recover a Blefling we have fo lately loft; and are capable of any Undertaking, that gives the leaft hopes of forcing her from the Arms of the Man that has done our Paffion the Injuftice: Nay we even imagine it a point of Honour to fupplant a Rival, preferr'd to her Favour, at the Expence of our Happinefs: Love heightens by the many Obftacles it finds; nor are the Rigours of a falfe Miftrefs, powerful enough to blunt its Edge. A Lover even flatters himfelf, that his continual Sollicitations, and the redoubled Eagernefs of his Paffion will regain a Heart, on which Conqueft his entire Happinefs depends.

Pray Sir, reply'd the Countefs, no more Apologies. We can now boaft of no fuch Martyrs to to Love, nor even read of 'em but in Romances. That Time's paſt, when a Lover's utmoſt Ambition conſiſted in triumphing over a Heart, inſenſible and inacceſſible to a Lover's Sighs. Our Love's but of a ſhort Date, without a ſuitable Return, or at leaſt of a fair Probability of Time's being more propitious to our Paſſion. A Friend of yours has very wittily hinted this in ſome Verſes imatating *Horace*. They run thus,

I.

Let others think the Glory great,
To conquer a coy Lady ſcar'd with Love:
 A ſingle Day my Nymph ſhall prove,
And as in Battle, I'll ſoon know my Fate:
The leaſt Impediment, and my Flame dies,
Nor will I long diſpute uncertain Joys;
 The greateſt Pleaſures I diſdain,
 When they muſt purchas'd be with Pain.

II.

My Heart could never long perſiſt
 Bound to a cruel Fair;
The Chace if it fatigues I ſoon deteſt;
 The flying Nymph may ſpare
 Her pains, in running out of reach;
I dread the Sea, and ſafe remain upon the Beach.

III.

A too wiſe Beauty, or too auſtere Prude,
One that continually hints Noble Blood,
Shall never be the Object of my Vows;
Give me a yielding Girl that's plain and free;
 My honeſt Amorous Heart allows,
 All Tranſports there included be;
 She ſhall reign Empreſs in my Heart,
 She ſhall reign all in every part.

Now Sir, continu'd the Counteſs, you muſt allow this to be the perfect Character of our

Modern

Modern Lovers; your Friend has difcover'd the very Secrets of their Hearts, and given us a very true Defcription of their Sentiments.

Indeed, Madam, reply'd another Lady, inftead of faying more than he ought, he has not depos'd the whole Truth: For it is daily evident, that a Lover's Inconftancy frequently anticipates that of their Miftreffes; they are. fo hafty and fo willing at the fame time, that they have feldom occafion to make the Reflections *Ovid* advifes to in favour of a Rupture.

(Do yet more to difengage your felf; reprefent her more faulty than fhe really is; fay fhe's Old, Short-wafted; and that her Breaft, the ufual fomenter of Love in others, raifes difguft; that fhe's neither graceful, nor handfome, tho' in effect fhe may excel in both. If fhe's Brown imagine her Tawny; if Fair, heideoufly Pale; If fhe be Lufty, fancy her puffed up with Fat; if of a juft height, and free Air, fay fhe's lean to the laft degree. Call her *Coquet*, fhould fhe be witty, brisk and full of Life; and if on the contrary fhe proves fober and difcreet, fancy her a meer *Agnes*.)

You fpoke very juftly Madam, reply'd the Countefs's Neice, when you hinted how ufelefs this Precept would prove to the Lovers in this Age, who without fuch Shifts have lately found an admirable Receipt for dead'ning their Miftreffes Charms: The Charms of a new one I mean. This laft Paffion fuborns, weakens, and at laft totally deftroys the Power of the firft.

This is not effected fo foon as you imagine, Madam, reply'd Sir *W*———, one Paffion is not fo eafily extinguifh'd by the Succeffion of another; nor is it always in our Power to ceafe loving; but on the contrary it proves often ufelefs to make thefe Reflections: Should they create

any

any small Distaste, the Advantage would be confiderable. There must be Beauty effective or imaginary to charm us, and our Passion will certainly cease when we can persuade our selves that she is no longer amiable.

But is that possible, interrupted another Gentleman? Are a Lover's Eyes so far open as to find any fault in the Person he adores? No, all's pleasing in her; all's agreeably ravishing, and it is a true saying, that there never was a disagreeable Object of Love. It seems as tho' the Eyes had repos'd all Confidence in the Heart as to judging of the Beauties of the Fair One; which being entirely devoted to Love, finds her all Charming; and studies to represent her in all her Perfections, the better to justifie the Choice he has made, and the Passion he so willingly indulges.

Really Sir, reply'd a Lady, I can by no means be of your Opinion in this Point. I'm sensible a Lover prepossess'd in his Mistress's Favour will not perceive those Defects, a more indifferent Person might; but there are some so visible, that it is impossible but he must see 'em, be he never so blind. A real Beauty indeed uses all her Endeavours to skreen 'em; but a Lover that is really willing to shake off his Chains, must strive to unmask her, as earnestly as she does the contrary. Thus *Ovid* advises.

(Proceed yet farther: Give her even your own Assistance to displease you, and put her upon doing those Things she is wholly ignorant of, that her Defects may appear more visible. Should she have a bad Voice, press her to sing; and if you fancy her Dancing yet more disagreeable, use your utmost endeavour to persuade her to Dance: If she has an Impediment in her Speech, or expresses her Thoughts amiss, hold her

her in a long Difcourfe: If fhe has an ill Gate, keep her Walking; and fhould a pair of Ruby Lips skreen a bad fet of Teeth, tickle her Fancy by diverting Stories, 'till an imprudent Laugh difcovers her Defects: In a word ufe all your Caprice to her Prejudice: weaken her Charms by difputing their Titles; and be as careful in difcovering her Defects, as fhe is diligent in concealing 'em.)

This is indeed, reply'd the Divine, the wholefomeft Precept *Ovid* has given us. In effect what is there more difagreeable, than to fee a Perfon act againft the Grain? Such Actions are fufficient to chill the moft ardent Flame: For there is really as much Vain-glory as Affection in Loving. A Lover applauds himfelf, when he fees the Perfon he adores have the Power of attracting the Eyes, and Efteem of all Beholders: He finds a fecret Vanity in it, and fancies that the Praifes daily heap'd on his Miftrefs, reflect in fome Meafure on himfelf. But on the contrary, he conceives a certain Diftafte, at every thing fhe does difagreeably; he partakes in the Shame; accufes her of Careleffnefs; reproaches himfelf with his bad Choice, and blufhes for the Imperfections of his Miftrefs.

You have carry'd it far enough Sir, interrupted a Lady, but take my Word, we are not fuch Fools as to commit the leaft Error in a Lover's Prefence that may give him the leaft Difguft. We know better how to manage ourfelves; and tho' we may be inclinable to flatter our own Perfections, yet we are not fo blind with Self-love as to be ignorant of our Defects: The Care we take to caft a Veil over 'em, makes it apparent, we are but too plainly convinc'd of 'em in our Hearts. I am of Opinion then, that a young

Lady

Lady will never Dance before her Lover, if she knows herself uncapable of performing answerable to his Expectation. He may give himself the Trouble to intreat, but the more he urges, the more cautious she'll be in complying; so that if this be the only Method of hating, he is in great danger of continuing a Lover.

The Lady is certainly in the Right, reply'd a Gentleman, the Fair Sex is much more curious in this Point than ours; and a Lover is so far from gaining by his Charmer's Defects, that he is seldom or never acquainted with 'em. You may tell the most ridiculous Stories in Nature, and they shall have no more Effect on Madam B—— than a Lecture of *Seneca*; she never opens her Lips, because she's sensible of the Advantage in keeping the Secret from taking Air: The most diverting Comedies are dull with her, and the *Italians* are no more than a parcel of mimicking Buffoons; her Reasons are very obvious. Madam U—— who naturally has a bad Complexion, manages with great Skill, a false Beauty when she comes in Company: And Madam T—— whose Gate is as disagreeable, as the rest of her Person is charming, has always some Pretext for not walking: She hates the Park as much as Madam C—— admires it, conscious of the gentle Air she always walks with. I could cite a thousand more Examples, but I remember we ought to spare our Neighbours. Besides——

We are sufficiently convinc'd Sir, said the Countess, of the Truth of what you alledge. Let us hear if the following Precept will be more agreeable: And then I'll give you my Word I'll have done.

(It may not be amiss to surprize the Fair One in her Chamber before the addition of Art to her natural

natural Beauty; for she may appear young and handsome when drest, who in her *Dishabille* proves quite otherwise; the Ornaments of Cloaths impose not a little on a Lover's Eyes, when a Person is more beholden to Art than Nature for her Charms. Nevertheless this Rule is not without its Exceptions; a careless Beauty has more powerful Charms; one may perceive in her negligent Air something so agreeable, as is not in the Power of rich Cloaths to add: Then the fewer Ornaments, the more enchanting.)

This is really true both ways, says Sir *W*—— an agreeable Negligence admirably well becomes a fine Women; but we have few such accomplish'd Beauties: It is evident ordinary Beauties have need of far-fetch'd additional Ornaments; and the Number of these undoubtedly surpasses that of the others. I know some Ladies really agreeable when dress'd, who could not avoid giving disgust when undress'd; so I think *Ovid* much in the Right when he advises us to surprize 'em in the Morning before they have borrow'd Charms from Patches, Paint and Wardrobe: Then we may see 'em unamiable, and their visible Imperfections will prove our Defence against their Inroads: For as I mention'd before, we are less taken with the Woman than her Beauty, that's the Source of our Love, that causes it to persevere, and the moment her Beauty begins to take Wing, our Passion finding no longer Allurement, is not tardy in following.

We are sensible of that, interrupted the Countess, and are but too well persuaded of the Injustice of your Sex in this Point. If they'd but suffer their Reason to govern their Passions, our Beauty would not be the only Cause of their Perseverance: They would admire Charms less subject

ject to Decay; I mean those of the Mind; and as these are never defac'd, but grow with us, we should always be in a Capacity of pleasing: But few Lovers have this Delicacy of Taste, they are more flatter'd, by the Desire of pleasing their Senses, than gratifying their Minds; they are Strangers to the more refin'd Flames of Love, the Delight of sublime Souls, and their Love is ordinarily fix'd on certain Charms which they are Slaves to, no longer than the Caprice lasts. For this reason we ought not to blam'd, for the Pains we take to preserve, or add to our Charms; we are sensible they are caught in Beauty's Net, and we are forc'd to attack 'em on their weakest side.

We by no means condemn, Madam, the just Care you have of your Beauty, reply'd a Gentleman, it well deserves the Pains you are at; and demands your utmost Application: Nature has given your Sex that Advantage over us, and you ought to make use of it; nor can we with Justice blame you for preserving so carefully a Treasure, capable of attracting the Eyes and Hearts of half the World. Our Satyr extends only to those who are negligent of their Charms, and by the little care they take for their Preservation, shew themselves unworthy of 'em. There are some never drest but upon making a Visit, and are so disagreeable at home, that a sight of 'em alone is sufficient to disgust the keenest Appetite. These are the Ladies *Ovid* advises us to surprize; nor is his Counsel to be rejected: More than one Lover has found his Account in it, and for my part, did I love to never so violent a pitch, it would prove the only Remedy, capable of effecting my Cure.

Your

Your Wound muſt be very Superficial then, reply'd a Lady, when ſuch a weak Remedy can effect a Cure, and reſtore you to your former ſtate of Health. However let us deſcant no more on a Topick ſo extremely diſadvantageous to our Sex; appoint one to continue the Subject to morrow, and let's retire.

The Perſon was nam'd, and the Company departed not a little ſatisfy'd with their *Second Entertainment*.

The Third ENTERTAINMENT.

AS ſoon as all the Company was ſeated, a young Lady, Niece to the Counteſs, who had the Night before borrow'd the Tranſlation in Proſe to read; began the Diſcourſe and ſaid: *Ah! what charming Thoughts am I fraught with? But they ought by no means to raiſe my Vanity; I accidentally fell into the moſt agreeable Precepts in the World; and eſpecially the firſt.* I'm almoſt perſuaded theſe Gentlemen will be of my Mind.

(If a Lover againſt his Will labours in the Quarries of a Stony Heart, let him ſtifle his Paſſion by a new one, or if it agrees better with his Inclinations, let him become a general Lover; 'tis the only certain way of ſhaking off his Chains; we become inſenſible of the Torments of Love, when we have arriv'd to the Knack of ſharing 'em. Apply this Remedy, and every Day will leſſen your Paſſion. Love ſeverally; for the only way to deſtroy one Paſſion is to engage in another.)

Well Sir, continu'd ſhe, addreſſing herſelf to one of the Gentlemen, does not this Remedy ſuit

suit the generality of Men; and is it not most opportune and easy?

Not at all Madam, reply'd he, of all the Remedies *Ovid* has prescrib'd, this seems to me the most difficult to Experience. Believe me Madam, it is not so easy to change your Affections, and mould your Heart at Pleasure. Has not *Ovid* himself inform'd us, that when Love has once fix'd his Empire in a Heart, it is impossible to dislodge him. It is not in our Power to eradicate a Passion fortify'd by Perseverance; and especially when it proves *Cupid*'s first Essay: A Friend of mine has writ a small Piece on this Subject, which would certainly convince you of what I say: He proves in effect, that the first Passions are most difficult to remove, and a Lover must suffer much Torment, before he can expect to gain his Point. A Heart that never lov'd before, loves with greatest Ardour; such a Lover gives himself entirely up to the Command of those Eyes that charm him, and strives to fill the *Vacuum* of his immense Desires: He lies open to those Charms he is so eager for, and in such Cases, Love makes the deepest Impressions: These first Amours are always most violent; Time can hardly extinguish 'em; Death alone totally eradicate 'em; and a Heart thus prepossess'd, retains with vast Delight, the Object of his first Desires.

Don't you think, Madam, my Friend's Expressions are much more just on this Head than *Ovid*'s, and the Precept of the one less certain than the other's Moral?

I'm of this Gentleman's Opinion, reply'd Sir *W*———, and I must needs add, that this Precept of *Ovid*'s is as useless as impracticable. Whence can proceed the saving Health from a
Re-

Remedy, that for avoiding one Evil plunges us into another? *Ovid* advises us to vary our Love; suppose it possible, or that we had really effected this difficult Task; can he give Security that this second Amour shall prove more successful than the First? How can we be assur'd that the Yoak, we by his Advice willingly take up, will be less uneasy, and intolerable than that we have shook off? Can he warrant the Success of so doubtful a Matter? Has *Cupid* reveal'd to him what we are likely to suffer?

What you alledge Sir, seems very reasonable, reply'd a Lady, but yet I don't find it so very difficult to answer you. If you'll only be at the pains of thoroughly examining *Ovid*'s Words you'll find he does not advise a second Passion, with design of subverting the First, but that you may love universally; have undetermin'd and roving Thoughts; and in a word *Coquet* it in all Places: In this Sense his Advice is both just and useful. For after all, it is but too plain, that these profess'd Lovers, their Hearts continually open to the Insult of powerful Charms, by loving too much, love in effect nothing: And if *Ovid* may rise in Justification of himself; he advises the Fair Sex to give no Attention to the Amorous Expressions of these Rovers: I took particular notice of this Place, because I thought it remarkable.

(Fly these Rovers, whose exuberant Love is still repeating to you what thousands have before experienc'd; whose easy Hearts feign a Passion for every Beauty they meet, and in effect love none.)

Those then who would free themselves from the Tyranny of a Mistress, must be of the number of profest Lovers; but in my Opinion those can

can be nothing more averse to true Love than the Coquetry he advises to.

You are really in the right, Madam, reply'd the Divine, and have perfectly comprehended *Ovid*'s Sense; but a Man of Honour can by no means personate this Part; it is properly the Character of young hair-brain'd Fellows, who according to the Modern *Horace*, have no Occupation, but drinking Tea all Day with the Ladies, and under Covert of a fair full-bottom'd Whig, plaguing 'em with their faint languid Passions.

Well Sir, reply'd a Lady, if you're of Opinion there must be a spice of Folly in obeying the preceding Precept; I am persuaded you will agree with me in this, that a Man must be very wise and arm'd with a great share of prudent Forecast, to come up to the Rules of the following.

(How violent soever your Passion prove, keep it secret; and appear all Ice before its charming Cause. When Tumults begin to discompose your Breast, affect a careless Gaiety, lest she perceive herself the fatal Cause. Never sigh in her Presence, but the more your Love encreases, the greater ought your Endeavours prove to stifle it: You will thus one Day effectually master what you first design'd. A Heart easily accustoms it self not to Love, the Fire extinguishes by not suffering it to blaze out; and he will at last prove no Lover, who has for a long time affected the being so.)

You spoke to the Purpose, Madam, reply'd Sir *W*———, when you said this Precept would require more Phlegm than Blood in the Constitutions of its Followers. A *Spaniard* perhaps might agree to it; but I am certain, neither an

Eng-

English nor *Frenchman* can make use of it. Tel me, continu'd he, what Lover can have so much command over himself? He that has, I'm certain can be no Lover. *Ovid* says, we become indifferent by the continual Affectation of Indifference; but I, in Opposition maintain, our Love rather increases, by affecting not to Love: Truth always precedes instead of following the Counterfeit; and it is impossible to pretend not to Love, unless we have once lov'd. Love is not so easily conceal'd, 'tis a Flame will discover it self, an Action, a Look, a very nothing betrays it, and the Pains we take to hide it, often tend to no other Effect than making it more apparent. *Cowley*, who was but too sensible of the Effects of Love, acknowledges this in the following Lines.

Men without Love, have oft so cunning grown,
  That something like it they have shown;
But none who had it, ever seem'd t'have none.

Love's of a strangely open, simple kind,
  Can no Arts, or Disguises find,
But thinks none sees it, 'cause it self is blind.

The very Eye betrays the inward smart,
  Love of himself left there a Part;
When thorough it, he pass'd into the Heart.

Or if by Chance the Face betray not it,
  But keep the Secret wisely, yet,
Like Drunkenness, into the Tongue 'twill get.

What you say Sir, is generally speaking true; but assure your self the contrary often happens: Looks, Actions, nay the Tongue is now no longer

ger the Interpreter of our secret Thoughts: We have an admirable Method of disguising our Sentiments, and Dissimulation is now the reigning Art. Hatred is a Passion no less violent than Love; nevertheless, don't we every Day meet Persons, who in their Hearts are our Mortal Enemies, and let load us with Acts of Generosity and Marks of Friendship; which, were we not acquainted with the Reasons for their pretended Kindness, might in all probability deceive us? Thus every one has a particular Aim, all their Actions drive at. *Tircis* feigns an extreme Passion for *Climene*, tho' every one easily perceives the Disguise; however he has his Reasons. *Damon*, on the contrary seems indifferent toward *Iris*, and really adores her; he too shews his Reasons: He fancies his pretended Indifference will make him more esteem'd, and that his Mistress perceiving his Coldness, will in Opposition become passionately in love with him.

True Sir, interrupted a Lady; and it is the Effect *Ovid* proposes from his following Precept.

(Whatever your Mistress says or does, never complain, nor seem displeas'd: Should she appoint a Rendezvous, fail not, and if she disappoints you, ne'er seem discompos'd: The hour once past, stay not a moment longer: And at your next Visit take no Notice, nor shew any signs of being vext: This is a most important Point. Avoid even talking of your Disappointment, and appear as Gay and Airy as usual; endeavour only to make her sensible how ready you are to quit your Chains, and that she has no longer the absolute Power over you, she could once boast of: The better to curb her Pride feign some your self, and urge it so far, as to make her believe you can even despise her:

This

This Method will excite her Love, and sufficiently prove how wholesom this Remedy really is.)

I can't comprehend what *Ovid* means by this, answer'd the Countess, his Book proposes Remedies for Love, and here he instructs us in loving. This last Advice tends rather to inspiring a Lady with Love, than to the Cure of a Lover already wounded; in my Mind this is most irregular. But I easily excuse him, when I reflect on the Difficulty of suppressing the Inclinations, Nature excites us to. *Ovid* was naturally Amorous; here his Heart betrays his Wit, and by an Error frequent with Lovers, endeavouring to write in Prejudice of Love, he writes in its Favour.

Very likely Madam, reply'd the Divine; but we may justify this last Precept of *Ovid*, by what he deposes at the beginning of his Treatise.

(If, says he, you love, and are equally belov'd, may your Flame ever continue, and may all your Pleasure consist in cherishing it: But if you suffer against your Will, in a cruel fair-one's Bondage, to save you from impending Ruin; I offer my Art.)

You see, Madam, by this, continu'd he, these Love Recipe's are not design'd for every one, tho' in effect he gains his Point here too; when he undertakes the easing a Lover's Pains, by making him belov'd by her, whose Rigour was his only Torment.

That's not what amazes me, reply'd Sir W———, 'tis this pretended Indifference he would have a Lover arm himself with, at the Sight of his Charmer: I still persist in maintaining the Impossibility of this. Let a Man be never so much Master of himself, he can never disguise his Passions so subtilly, as not to be seen thro', especially in Love. Ah! what is there so void of Art, as a Heart truly passionate? All its Precautions are useless; Love will appear in spite of Opposition, and it must be allow'd much easier not to love, than to conceal a Passion once entertain'd. The History of *Clidamas* and young *Doris* will be a convincing Proof of it. If Madam, addressing himself to the Countess's Neice, you will pardon my interrupting the Sequel of your Precepts, I'll give it you in as few Words as possible.

With all my Heart, reply'd the Lady, and that you mayn't be too hasty in reciting this Adventure, let me tell you, I have finish'd all I design'd to say: I had the Assemblies Permission, to express my Thoughts; I made use of my Priviledge, and now, Sir, you have the liberty of saying what you please; while I give you all the Attention you can demand.

Sir *W*—— immediately began this pleasant Adventure, in the following manner.

The History of CLIDAMAS and Young DORIS.

IT is certain nothing conduces more to mutual Engagements of Friendship, than Neighbourhood; nor is it less instrumental in Matters of Love; whoever has heard of *Pyramus* and *Thisbe*, must be sufficiently convinc'd of this. *Clidamas* was young *Doris*'s Neighbour, had frequent Opportunities of seeing her, laught, toy'd, walk'd with her, and diverted her with a thousand pretty Fooleries; but it is evident he had no design of loving, tho' *Doris* interrupted it
other-

otherwife. She was willing to impute, to a Paffion for her, what was but the Effects of *Clidamas*'s gallant Humour; and fancying herfelf belov'd, infenfibly engag'd her Heart in a Paffion for him: This Error caus'd her Love to perfevere, and fortify'd it every Day in his Favour; who was ftill cruelly infenfible of the many Overtures fhe daily made. Her Looks, Actions, every thing manifefted the fecret Inclinations of her Heart. But *Clidamas* us'd no Endeavours for underftanding a Language he never profefs'd; and as we are not eafily perfuaded of the Paffion of one, we have no real Inclination for our felves: *Clidamas* never gave himfelf the trouble of enquiring into the Proceedings of the Amorous *Doris*. However, fhe ftill lov'd, and the pains fhe was at to conceal her Paffion, made it more violent. Any other but fhe would have had the Courage to break the Ice firft, and at the Expence of a few Blufhes, which would have augmented her Charms, confefs'd a Paffion, not even thought of by the Perfon belov'd. But fhe was young and unexperienc'd, nor had the Confidence, or Addrefs to make fuch a Confeffion. Her Modefty check'd the Offers her Love would have oblig'd her to make, and fhe was not a little difcompos'd thro' her Irrefolution. However, fhe ftill lov'd, was filent, and the Conftraint fhe was under in concealing the Secret, threw her into a languifhing Melancholy, which was foon follow'd by a violent Fever. Let us now leave *Doris*, oblig'd to keep her Bed; and bring upon the Stage a young Actor, who is to prove the chief Intriguer in the Plot: 'Tis *Clidamas*'s Brother, between Nine and Ten Years of Age, handfome, fprightly, and of a brisk Wit, fuch as is very taking in

D 4   Chil-

Children of his Years. He was often with *Doris*; and as he found her very agreeable, frequently call'd her his Mistress, and would often in Jesting, say, how much he ador'd her. Hearing she was now sick, he thought himself oblig'd as a Lover to make her sensible by a Letter, how great a share he bore in her Illness; he accordingly writ the following one, and sent it by a Footman to his pretended Mistress.

BILLET.

I Protest, my Dear Doris, *I am not a little concern'd for your Indisposition. Did your Cure depend on me, I would not see you long languish, but to restore your Health, would most willingly share your Affliction; nor could my Sufferings then be comparable to those I now endure, by being depriv'd of your Company: The Days are doubly tedious, and I am no longer Master of my usual Gaiety. For God's sake, my Dear* Doris, *endeavour a recovery, as soon as possible, unless you've a mind I should sympathize in your Illness. I will certainly see you after Dinner. Adieu.*

Clidamas.

I leave you to judge the agreeable Surprize our fair one was in at reading this Letter; for lest you mayn't comprehend the Matter, give me leave to inform you, she was really of Opinion, her beloved *Clidamas* had sent it; nor could she undeceive herself, having never receiv'd one from him before; and being consequently ignorant of either his Characters or Stile. The better to express her Joy it was requisite she were sensible of a parallel one; the Violence of her Fever immediately was appeas'd, peas'd, and calling for Pen and Ink, she writ the following *Billet doux*, and sent it to her dearest *Clidamas*, by a Neighbour, in whom she put great Confidence.

Her ANSWER.

NO, my Dear Clidamas, *I can no longer be ill, since you seem to have so great a share in what concerns me. You might have easily spar'd me the Pains I have lately undergone, had you but made this Confession sooner. Ah! why was you so long silent? And was it possible all my Actions should not inform you, how dear you was to me? You certainly could not doubt my Passion. A hundred times have I design'd explaining my self, and as often by I know not what Modesty, peculiar to my Age and Sex, have been forc'd against my Inclinations to desist. But since You have made the first Overtures, it is no longer for me to dissemble. I love, Dearest* Clidamas, *and Love's the only cause of my Illness. Visit me as soon as possible, and confirm that Happiness in Words, which your Letter assures me of. With what Joy shall I hear you say,* Doris *I love you! I fancy the Excess of Pleasure will be fatal; but come. Adieu.*

Doris.

Never was Man more surpriz'd than *Clidamas*, at the receipt of this Letter. He was ignorant of the Accident that caus'd it; he read it over and over, and the oftner he read it, the more he was amaz'd. He knew not what to resolve upon, and was in no small Perplexity of Mind, to conclude whether he ought in Honour to visit her or not: At last he dertermin'd in the Affirmative, not so much with design of making

making ufe of *Doris*'s advances of Love; as to convince himfelf whether it was really directed to him. Accordingly he went, and having at entering her Chamber paid his Refpects, feated himfelf in an Eafy-Chair near the Bed-fide, ftill irrefolute how to proceed. He had not the Confidence, tho' it was his only defign in coming, to inform himfelf of the Matter, and refolv'd on a fatal Silence, which threw *Doris* into the utmoft defpair. She certainly expected a quite different Treatment from one whofe Letter had exprefs'd fo violent a Paffion: They both had a defire to fpeak, but neither had the Confidence. At laft *Doris*, who was willing to interpret *Clidamas*'s Silence and Diforder to his Advantage, which the good Opinion fhe had of herfelf was the Caufe of, firft broke their long Silence, and in a faint languifhing Tone ask'd him, if he had receiv'd her Letter? *Clidamas*, by this convinc'd of his being the Perfon mention'd in the *Billet*, was more furpriz'd than before, and had fcarce the Courage to anfwer, yes, Madam, I receiv'd it. If you, reply'd *Doris*, receiv'd it, how is it poffible you can appear fo infenfible? Where are all thofe Tenderneffes, and paffionate Expreffions your Letter abounds with? Mine, Madam, interrupted *Clidamas*, full of Amazement! Whence this Surprize, reply'd fhe? Oh! you now begin to repent your having encourag'd a Paffion, which was the only Caufe of your Letter? *Clidamas*, altogether ignorant of the Matter, imagin'd the Violence of the Fever had made her Delirious, and infenfible of what fhe faid. Pardon me, Madam, reply'd he, if I take the liberty to tell you, you are miftaken in the Perfon: Open your Eyes, Madam, continu'd he, and be affur'd you are now talking

ing to *Clidamas*. I am sensible, Ingrate, reply'd she, with an Air, that argu'd equal Love and Anger, that I am now talking to *Clidamas*; let him satisfy himself, he is now discoursing with the same *Doris* he sent this Letter to in the Morning: She was just about taking the Letter out of her Bosom, when *Clidamas*'s little Brother enter'd the Chamber. Well my pretty Mistress, says he, with a joyful Air, how do you find your self in Health now? And pray how do you like the Letter I took the Liberty to send you in the Morning? *Doris* at hearing these Words was ready to die with shame; she stifled the bitter Reproaches she intended for her young Lover, and was oblig'd to seek in silence, a Remedy for her troubled Mind. *Clidamas* to spare her the Confusion his Presence must necessarily put her in, quitted the Chamber, and defer'd till another Opportunity, his Duty in comforting her for so fatal a Mistake: For I have been inform'd since, that he thought in Honour he ought not to see her in continual Pain for the Advances, an excess of Passion had forc'd her to make; that on this Consideration he had recompenc'd her Love, by entertaining a like Passion, and that they now enjoy all the Pleasures of a mutual Love.

Really, reply'd the Countess, I am not a little satisfy'd at the happy Catastrophe of *Doris*'s Passion, and I confess I was mightily concern'd for its Success: I should have entertain'd an ill Opinion of *Clidamas*, had he still been so much Master of himself as not to shew a Lady some Favour, whose Love was so entirely fix'd on him.

You see by this Adventure, continu'd Sir *W*———, how impossible it is to conceal a Passion

on once grown abſolute; or to affect an Indifference maugre our Inclinations.

I'm of your Opinion, reply'd the Counteſs, and I fancy *Doris* agrees with us both in this Point. But I perceive it is almoſt time to retire homewards: Let us break up the Aſſembly, and before Supper divert our ſelves at *Ombre*: The Company agreed to the Propoſal and retir'd.

The Fourth ENTERTAINMENT.

THE Pleaſures of the Mind have this Advantage over the more ſenſual Delights, that they never cloy nor are accompany'd by thoſe ſurfeiting Diſguſts, which are the conſtant Concomitants of the others; but the very Enjoyment of theſe enhances the deſire of repeating 'em. It is no wonder then to find our witty Aſſembly ſo eager for a Rendezvous, which deluded the Minutes ſo agreeably. The Gentleman that was to begin the Diſcourſe, was none of the laſt there; and ſeeing every one ſeated, ſaid, Gentlemen and Ladies, I have acquitted myſelf to the utmoſt of my Power of the Charge enjoin'd me; where if I have not ſucceeded, the Fault is entirely my own. Another might perhaps object the little time he had to prepare himſelf; but I muſt confeſs I had to ſpare. In my Opinion there needs not much leiſure to reflect on any Subject; 'tis a Work that demands the firſt Flights of Wit; when Thoughts are work'd up with Labour; the Property is alter'd, and it renders 'em unvaluable; ſince they are ſtrip'd of thoſe Charms, a happy Unaffectedneſs would give

give 'em. I hope Ladies you'll pardon this Preamble; I am sensible you come for no other end but commenting on *Ovid*'s Precepts. I'll now endeavour to satisfy you by the following one.

(Lovers that are willing to free your selves from your Malady, fly Solitude; it increases, or at least nourishes the Pains of Love. Instead of sequestring your self from, entertain all Company; and select some Friends, who may endeavour to divert the Torments, Love is the subtle Cause of.)

This Precept is perfectly good, says a Lady, for I am really of Opinion, nothing can be more dangerous to a Lover than Solitude, nor any Advice preferable to that for avoiding it. The Forests, Rivers and Fountains, have I know not what in 'em that naturally inspires Love and tender Thoughts; nor do I at all wonder at the Poets feigning *Cupid* to be born in the Woods: There he made those Laws, since grown so universal: There he first let flie his Arrows at Mankind: And it was there he first laid the Plan of those Chains, which have since enslav'd our Souls. Shepherds were first sensible of his Power; they first built Altars to their new Deity; they eccho'd his Fame throughout the Earth, and celebrated his Honour in strains of Poetry. Since when, Love has haunted the Woods; and those Places he so long honour'd with his Presence, retain even at this time a secret Virtue of insinuating Love. The Flames he so often fomented there, are not so utterly extinguish'd, but there yet remains some Sparks, capable of enflaming a too daring Heart; and those Trees whose Barks are still Witnesses of many amorously intervoven Cyphers, seem now to invite Lovers to the like Diversions.

You are in the right, Madam, reply'd the Divine, Love has a ſtrange Inclination for Solitude; and it is a vaſt Satisfaction to a Lover, that he can complain of the Cruelty of his Charmer, tho' to the inſenſible Rocks. He looks upon them as Witneſſes and Confidents of his amorous Soliloquies, and paſſionate Anxieties; and is pleas'd in making to them his amorous Complaints. But, ah! how fatal is this Pleaſure? It obliges Lovers to indulge Solitude, and it is that alone ruins 'em. The unhappy Liberty they enjoy in venting their Grief, does but make 'em more wretched, and plunges 'em deeper in the dangerous Abyſs, whence they endeavour to extricate themſelves. Converſation of jocular Friends alone is able to divert their ſad melancholy Reflections, and render 'em leſs attentive to their Evil. But theſe Friends muſt be true; altogether devoted to our Intereſts; equally Sharers of our Mirth and Sorrow; and in a word our better half. A Lover muſt ſeek in their ſolid Diſcourſes, a Remedy, or at leaſt an Amuſement for his Paſſion; this is the true Uſe of Friendſhip; this is . . . . .

Hold, Sir, reply'd the Counteſs, let me beg of you to urge your Morals no farther. If a Friend has no other Office, but the comforting an amorous Friend, we ſhall run the Riſque of having no Friend; and Friendſhip would be baniſh'd the Earth, as altogether uſeleſs, had it no other end than this. Believe me, Sir, continu'd ſhe, thoſe Ages are paſt, when deſpairing Lovers hang'd themſelves at their Miſtreſſes Doors; that ungenteel Faſhion is no longer *a-la-mode*, or to ſpeak more properly never was. The preſent Age is ſo deprav'd, that a Perſon would be ridicul'd, that ſhould but make the

leaſt

least mention of dying for Love; and would, like the *Phœnix*, be accounted the Miracle of Caprice. No, Lovers refign themfelves now-a-days entirely to their Stars; they are meer Philofophers in this Point, and prepar'd for all manner of Accidents. They have forgot to importune the Forefts with their Sighs, and Eccho with their Groans and Complaints; they are in effect utterly void of the Art of tiring the *Grotto's* with their melancholy and amorous Soliloquies.

You rally us, Madam, fays a Gentleman, but take care Love does not punifh you for your fatyrical Wit, by throwing in your way the very Man you have fo pertly defcrib'd, and at the fame time, oblige you to love him. Then perhaps you may confefs, the Remedies you now make fo light of, are not fo ufelefs as you imagine; and may then give us your Opinion of the Dangers of Solitude to an amorous Heart. Grant Love my Prophecy may never come true, and that you may ever be deftitute of a Paffion, wherein either the preceding or following Remedies may be of ufe.

(Thou that endeavour'd to avoid loving, fhun all Lovers Company; every thing advifes you to it; and after the Example of a once amorous Friend, flie 'em. You'll hear nothing all Day, but tender Difcourfes, capable only of awakening in your Heart the Paffion you are endeavouring to fhake off. Love is contagious and communicative; the little Deceiver by engaging your Attention to other Perfons foft Arguments, gains admittance to your Heart.)

This is moft ufeful Counfel, fays the Divine, and founded on Experience. We are eafily tainted with the Vices or Vertues of thofe we converfe with, and their Examples good or bad,
make

make deep Impreſſions on our Minds. Gameſters naturally incline us to Gaming; while the more profitable Company of the learned Few, inſpires us with a Deſire of becoming ſuch; and he that can find Charms therein, will ſoon augment their Number: Such is the Weakneſs of the generality of Men; we conform our ſelves to our Friends, and are complaiſant even to ſuch a degree as to bluſh at being backward in imitating their greateſt Vices. A *young Spark* is aſham'd of being behind-hand in Love, when his amorous Companions are continually rallying him for his fooliſh Indifference; ſo that he is oblig'd, either to love like them, or leave their Company. If then 'tis dangerous for indifferent Perſons to frequent Lovers Company, how much more is it ſo, to thoſe, who languiſh under the remains of a violent Paſſion? Their dying Flame is ſoon recover'd; their Wounds are eaſily renew'd; and they quickly entangle themſelves in the Snares, they ſo lately endeavour'd to ſhake off.

You reaſon very juſtly Sir, anſwer'd a Lady, and it ſeems to me as tho' that Perſon had but half renounc'd the Pleaſures of Love, who can be pleas'd in the Company of Inamorato's entirely devoted to 'em. He ſhews by that the remains of tenderneſs in his Soul; that it is with the greateſt Regret he abandons the Happineſs of loving, and of being belov'd; and that the Charmer, whoſe Authority he endeavours to diſpute, has yet Poſſeſſion of his Heart. He feels an inexpreſſible Pleaſure, in being witneſs of the Paſſions of other Lovers; their Diſcourſes tickle his Imagination; he is pleas'd to ſee them enjoy a Happineſs he is ſo hardly depriv'd of, and which his Heart is ſo willing to entertain. Oh! in what danger is a Lover in ſuch a State?

State? How easily does he pass from desire to its Effects? He finds his pretended Indifference vanish insensibly, and he immediately concludes, a Life tho' unfortunately Amorous, much preferable to one past away in a tedious Indifference. To avoid this Evil, if one may be allow'd to call that an Evil, without which there is no pleasure in Life, he ought to shun Lovers Company, whose Examples make him inclinable to a Passion, he was once in a fair way of resisting.

At that rate, reply'd Sir *W*———, he must shun all young Gentlemen's Company in general; for they are all in general Lovers; his Friends must be all Men of Threescore or upwards; and he must have their Gravity at five and twenty. No, no, this Counsel can never be follow'd, for where ever we turn our Eyes Love triumphs: He possesses all young Hearts, he gives all the Entertainment to, and creates all the Business of the *Beau-monde*; so if a Man must avoid all Company that inclines that way, he may e'en go look for Diversion, with the Beasts of the Field. But hold, what do I say? The very Beasts themselves own his Soveraignty; and are equally sensible of his Power to subdue their natural Fierceness. *Ovid* assures us of this in his Art of Loving; and our Author of Precepts of Gallantry confirms it.

(The Sheep, says he, by its Bleeting calls its Companion; the Lyon roars, and the Bull bellows, thro' excess of Love: The Birds are sensible of *Cupid*'s Force, and the Fish burn even at the bottom of the Sea. So that in effect Love reigns universally.)

If according to these Precepts it be true, continu'd he, that every thing in Earth, Air and Sea,

Sea, is sensible of Love; how is it possible we can avoid Lovers Company? Where, pray, can proceed the Advantage of a Remedy, which it is impossible to make use of?

You take the meaning too literally Sir, answer'd the Countess, and if you call that Love which is really no more than a Gentleman-like Complaisance for our Sex in general, you misapply the Word. Love soars infinitely higher; you know it better than I, but you are so malicious you never speak your real Thoughts. You have your Aim too, you endeavour to decoy us, and make us fancy that the effect of Love, which only proceeds from a general Complaisance. But believe me, we are not so credulous in this Affair, as you may imagine; we have the Faculty of distinguishing those things you endeavour to confound. Let Mr. ——— be judge, I'm certain he must be on my side, if he would be just enough to espouse Truth, in prejudice to his own Interest.

We have no time, Madam, says he, to solve so nice a question, we can better employ it in other Matters.

I foresaw, reply'd the Countess, you'd avoid an Answer; but it signifies nothing, I'll still persist in my Opinion, 'till you have convinc'd me of the contrary. You may go on Sir, added she, I've done.

The Gentleman immediately continu'd the Discourse, with the following Precept.

(Carefully avoid the sight of your Charmer, lest a Glance from her Eyes renews your Wound; shun all Places she frequents; be yet more cautious; carry no Correspondence with her Domesticks, and above all avoid her Confident; You can never be too much upon your guard

against

againſt Love, ſince a Paſſion ill extinguiſh'd is eaſily blow'd up.)

Certainly, ſays the Counteſs, that Perſon muſt depend very much on his own Strength, that will run the hazard of ſeeing his Miſtreſs: He deceives and abuſes himſelf. Love ever ſollicitous to engage him more ſtrongly, gives him this vain Confidence in himſelf, and ſo ſhuts his Eyes, againſt the Ambuſcades laid for his Ruin. I have known ſome, who endeavouring to convince their Miſtreſſes of their having no command over them; take all Opportunities to be in their Company; ſeem to behold 'em with the ſame Coldneſs as other Beauties, and affect an Indifference they are perfect Strangers to; for it is evident they are, ſpite of their Vizards, Tributaries to *Cupid*. It is the Pleaſure of ſeeing 'em alone, makes 'em frequent their Company. The ſureſt way therefore is to avoid 'em; and Flight is the only Remedy to be made uſe of at ſuch a Juncture.

You ſay true Madam, anſwer'd another Lady; but this is not ſo ſoon done as ſaid. When one really loves, has one the Power of abſenting? No, we may endeavour it, but in vain. The Heart in ſuch Caſes mutinies againſt the Will, and we find our ſelves conſtrain'd by an imperceptible Force, to give full Scope to our Wiſhes. The Heart is rarely govern'd by the Mind, and a Lover finds himſelf at his Miſtreſs's Door, before he is ſenſible whither he was going; his Buſineſs lay otherways; Love leads him to his Charmer, and it is impoſſible for him not to obey its gentle Violence.

No one can deſcribe an irreſolute Lover, with greater Life than you have Madam, reply'd Sir W———; and the very accident you now mention is lately befel one of the greateſt Galants at Court; the moſt Amorous, and moſt belov'd; you may eaſily imagine who I mean. He lov'd Madam *v*———— even to Diſtraction, and indeed it was not poſſible for him to love, without a return of Paſſion. However theſe two Lovers had faln out; and ſuch little Love-broils are often the happy Cauſes of redoubling a Paſſion. He was a whole fortnight without ſeeing her; an Age to one that lov'd like him: He was really angry with his Miſtreſs, and was unwilling the World ſhould think he had made the firſt Advances towards a Reconciliation; he imagin'd her in the Wrong, and thought he could not in point of Honour comply firſt. By this means he committed a Violence on himſelf, the Torments of which, are eaſier to be felt, than expreſs'd. He was every moment tempted to viſit his fair One, and he as bravely reſiſted, 'till at laſt he accidentally yielded to the Importunity of his paſſionate Deſires. He went out one Day, deſigning nothing leſs than viſiting her, and his Foot-man aſking him where he would go, was unadviſedly anſwer'd to Madam *v*————; now admire the Power of Love; the Coach ſtop'd at the Door, and before he was ſenſible where he was, he found himſelf in her Chamber. She was alone, reſting herſelf on a Couch, in a very melancholy Poſture, as one full of Meditation. He was touch'd at the Sight, attentively beheld his Charming Counteſs, ſtill ſilent, tho' his Eyes ſufficiently ſpoke the Diſorders of his Mind. She gave him a look full of Grief and Love, and her Charms were, if poſſible, augmented by the Confuſion the Earl had put her in. Her Beauty! the languiſhing Air of her Eyes! a fortnights Abſence! Love!!

all

all thefe contributed to the height'ning her Lover's Paffion. He approaches her, throws himfelf at her Feet, grafps her foft Hand, bath's it with Tears, and giving himfelf entirely up to the Tranfports of his Love, fhews more tender and paffionate Proofs of a fervent Affection than ever.

This, continu'd Sir *W———*, is the Character of a true Lover; he gives himfelf up wholly to his Inclinations, and feeks a Peril that pleafes him; for he muft certainly love very moderately, who can for any time fhun his Beloved's Company.

I own it Sir, reply'd the Divine, and if you give your felf the trouble to examine *Ovid*'s Words more nicely, you'll find his Opinion agree with ours. He would not have us fhun a Lady, as we would a Lyon; he knows the Impoffibility of fuch a Performance; he only advifes us to ufe our Endeavours, and expofe our felves as little as poffible to their Eyes, nor willingly run the hazard of feeing 'em. He was not ignorant of the Weaknefs of an enamour'd Heart; he knew Love would triumph over Reafon; and that a Look from our fair One would be able to deftroy our firmeft Refolutions. It is on thefe Conditions he prefcribes our Abfence; and in my Opinion his Counfel is founded on very good Reafons.

There's no one doubts it, reply'd a Gentleman, nor do I believe the following one lefs reafonable.

(Thou Lover, who art willing to quit thy Bondage, conceal the Caufe from publick Knowledge. The fureft way to ftifle your Paffion, is to be filent; for what one Day can extinguifh, another may very probably reftore. Above all no revealing. A Lady, who once has had the Power to pleaſe, never finds a ſevere Judge, and can eaſily juſtifie herſelf. Whatever Proofs you may have to convince her, a favourable Word alone on her ſide turns their Edge, and the moſt unreaſonable Arguments in Nature, are able to perſuade a credulous Lover. No revealing then.)

Without offence to *Ovid*, ſays the Counteſs, I think this way of proceeding very unjuſt. What? Would he have a Miſtreſs quitted, without ſo much as ſhewing Reaſons why? This is neither Fair nor Honourable; for in my Opinion it ſeems but reaſonable to hear, what can be alledg'd in favour of 'em, before final Condemnation. If this Precept was follow'd, our Sex would have very great Cauſe of complaining; We ſhould be the very May-game of our Lover's Caprice and Jealouſy; and be abandon'd upon the leaſt Suſpicion how groundleſs ſoever. They would be continually complaining, and we ſtill repreſented to their Minds, in worſe Colours than we really deſerve. We might object our Innocence, but that would ſtand us in little ſtead with them; ſince they'd baffle whatever we could ſay in our Juſtification, and not ſo much as let us have the Pleaſure of undeceiving 'em, or diſſipating their raſh and unjuſt Suſpicions. Was all your Sex, Sir, govern'd by Reaſon, Patience might be of ſome uſe to us; but there are ſome ſo unjuſt in Love, that it is impoſſible to hold even a two-days Correſpondence, in a manner ſuitable to the Buſineſs of Love. Witneſs the Capricious *Damon*. What Woman tho' never ſo fondly amorous, could comply with his eternal Caprice, and fantaſtical Humour? He is ſo unadviſedly Jealous, that he is even ſo of his own Shadow. His

His own Shadow, reply'd Sir *W*⸺; impossible!

His own Shadow, Sir, answer'd the Countess, and since you seem ignorant of this pleasant Adventure, I'll give it you in as few Words as possible.

The Comical History of DAMON; *Jealous of his own Shadow.*

Amon is a Person that carries his Jealousy to such an extreme, that his Example alone will be sufficient to condemn so unreasonable a Passion. He lov'd *Constantia*, and was belov'd by her: She was a Widow, had Wit and Beauty to an infinite degree. Many Persons of Quality were her Admirers, but she gave 'em no Encouragement, that *Damon*, who had design'd to marry her, might have no grounds for Jealousy; a failing he was naturally very much addicted to. He made her one time a Visit, and found her closely engag'd in Discourse with a very handsome young Gentleman, whom he had never before seen. The familiarity they discours'd with, was a sufficient Cause of *Damon*'s Chagrin, nor could his Love for *Constantia* hinder him from shewing very visible Marks of his Discontent. She soon perceiv'd it, and lest he might imagine her pleas'd at his Disorder, told him the Gentleman was a Brother of hers lately come from the Army. *Damon* prepossess'd with Jealousy, thought all she said no more than a cautious Artifice to deceive him; and having staid in the Chamber some few Moments, with the utmost disorder in his Countenance, retir'd; the better to consider of the Methods proper to resolve himself who this young Spark was; whom he imagin'd a Gallant of his Mistress's. He was soon inform'd of his being her real Brother; and tho' he was asham'd of his gross Mistake, yet he could not forbear, being very vigilant over *Lydamon*'s Proceedings, (for so was the Gentleman call'd) and using all his Endeavours to rob him of Opportunities to converse with his Sister. Nay he urg'd his Jealousy so far, as to beg the favour of her to admit him no more in her Company. *Constantia* was so complaisant as to oblige him, rather than see him so disturb'd by a Passion which daily augmented. Nevertheless all her Endeavours were ineffectual, to destroy his Suspicions. He imagin'd, she sacrific'd herself to the Happiness of a private Lover, and giving way to this unjust thought, one Evening continu'd his Visit to such an hour as oblig'd her to beg his Absence, that she might repose herself. He immediately did her the Injustice to believe she was urgent for his Departure, for the more convenient introducing some Gallant, she was in Expectation of; and full of their cursed Thoughts, reproach'd her a thousand times before he took his leave. As he quitted the Chamber, he saw accidentally his own Shadow, by the light of the Flambeaux; and yielding to his jealous Suggestions, without more a-do, fancy'd it some happy Rival, endeavouring to shun his Presence. This Thought, urg'd by his Curiosity to know what it really was, made him run down Stairs with more than ordinary Precipitation, the better to cut off his Rival in Imagination from the Door. The Footman, who held the Light, seeing him run down so hastily, and apprehensive he might stumble over him, put out the Flambeau, and so escap'd his

his Fury; whilſt *Damon* in making diligent ſearch, had got the Coach-man by the Collar, and almoſt ſtrangl'd him. The Fellow's Cries ſoon call'd together all *Conſtantia*'s Servants, who with one conſent fell upon *Damon*, and had almoſt kill'd him by their many and violent Blows; when their Miſtreſs appear'd. At ſight of her they immediately deſiſted; and gave *Damon* ſome reſpite to conſider his Miſtake, who aſham'd at his Folly, vow'd at his going out of the Houſe never to ſee her more.

You are now ſenſible, added the Counteſs, addreſſing herſelf to the Company, that Jealouſy had ſo entire a Power over *Damon*, that he was at laſt even Jealous of his own Shadow. At her repeating theſe Words they all burſt out a-laughing, 'till one of the Ladies interrupted this pleaſant Scene, and ſaid.

Damon is not the only Perſon has been troubled with the like Viſions; many Lovers are as ſubject to Jealouſy as he; nay very often too with as little Cauſe: Is it then reaſonable we ſhould bear with it? Ought not they to find Grounds for their Suſpicions, before they make all the World ſenſible of their Folly? And not accuſe their Miſtreſſes of Perfidy, 'till they are perfectly convinc'd of their being falſe. They ought moderately to ſhew their Reaſons, and urge the Wrong they have receiv'd; that they may have the Satisfaction of ſeeing their Miſtreſſes confounded, or juſtify'd.

I'm certain you'll agree with me, Madam, tho' I am of a different Opinion, reply'd Sir *W———*, in this Point. I muſt acknowledge, I think, this Enquiry too dangerous. *Ovid* ſays the ſame, and Experience ſhews Grounds for what he alledges. The Fair Sex have ſuch an
ad-

admirable knack of excuſing themſelves, that it is even impoſſible not to believe 'em: The firſt Apology of a Lady belov'd, argues her blameleſs; Nay, tho' ſhe confeſs her Crime, at the leaſt ſign of Repentance, we are overjoy'd that it is in our Power to pardon her; every thing ſpeaks in her favour, nor can the moſt incens'd Lover on Earth ſee two lovely Eyes drown'd in Tears, whether real or feign'd; but he muſt immediately forget all his former Reſentments. He begins by accuſing himſelf, thinks he is alone anſwerable for thoſe Tears he obliges her to ſhed, he is eaſily inclin'd to take the Fault on himſelf, and ask Pardon of one, whoſe only deſign was the obtaining his.

This is really, added a Gentleman, the uſual Method of proceeding with Lovers. I have ſeen ſome in the height of Reſentment, go with a fix'd Reſolution to reproach their Miſtreſſes, with their Falſhood; but no ſooner were they admitted to her Preſence, but they loſt all Power of Speaking. Their premeditated Reproaches dy'd between their Lips; and their Sighs, rather than Words, inform'd 'em, what Reaſon they had to complain. Indeed it is much ſafer to be thus ſilent, than urge a Reſentment too far, and make all the World acquainted with their Charmer's Perfidy. *Ovid* adviſes it in the following manner.

('Tis a Crime in Love to hate thoſe Beauties we have taken diſguſt at. 'Tis a Liberty allow'd to none but brutiſh Souls; and there is no Scandal comparable to that of two Lovers becoming Enemies. It often happens, that an exceſs of Anger forces us to defame the Perſons we have ador'd; and afterwards by Reconciliation attone for our heinous Fault; but Shame ſuc-
ceeds

ceeds all this. Fly then such Examples; and rather think of absolutely forgetting, than defaming her; nor dare profane a Temple, where you have once sacrific'd. Love is ill cur'd, when hatred must prove the Remedy; we daily see it; and Indifference is a much more advantageous Part to act; since excess of Hatred is often succeeded by an excess of Love, but Indifference never.)

This Precept, says a Lady, proceeds from a true Gentleman-like Spirit; and I am really angry with those Persons, who would intimate as tho' *Ovid*'s Inclinations were Knavish in Matters of Love; 'tis meer Slander. Nothing in the World can be more Honourable than this Precept, nor less observ'd. Our Modern Lovers are not so Scrupulous; and are discreet no longer than their Flame continues; that once extinguish'd, they are vain enough to boast of the smallest Favours, their Importunity has obtain'd. The least Disgust makes 'em forget their Duty, and discover what ought to be eternally secret. Their Love concludes in sudden Storms, and produces the most violent Effects, an inveterate hatred can be capable of. Thus they recompence their Charmer's Kindness, by the blackest of Ingratitude.

I can by no means justify this sort of Lovers, reply'd Sir *W——*, their Proceedings are base, and unworthy this honourable Moral, which all the World ought to be jealous of. But Ladies give me leave to tell you, the Fault lies often at your Door. Before you surrender your Hearts, you ought to consider the Merit of the Persons that lay Claim to it; and have a strict Eye on the Life and Conversation of a Man, that so willingly offers his own. You very often suffer

a young

a young giddy-brain'd Fop, to supplant a Man of Worth and Honour; you seem more captivated with the other's fantastical Airs, and affected Tittle, tattle, than the true Merit, and intrinsick Value of this; and are more easily engag'd by the Fop's empty Flames, than his Rival's real Passion, not set off with the modish Ornament of Expression; a Quality the other abounds with, tho' Love is the least of his Designs. This is the ordinary Vice of your Sex, and the Catastrophes of such inconsiderate Passions, are seldom free from Vexations. Thus Ladies, continu'd he, the better to prevent their Disorders, look before you leap, and be assur'd of your Lover's Merit, before you suffer him admittance to your Heart.

Pray Sir, how is that possible, interrupted a Lady? Men are so cunning grown, that even the most scrupulous may be deceiv'd, since there is no longer dependance, on outward Appearance, for the sincerity of the Heart; and since it is utterly impossible to read their inward Sentiments. Probabilities are deceitful, and there is nothing more resembles true Love, than a Passion well feign'd.

It may bear a Resemblance for some small time, reply'd a Gentleman, but the Mark will soon be discover'd, and you consequently be undeceiv'd. Heaven has given the Fair Sex an admirable Insight into the Soul, the better to distinguish the true from false Lovers; and it would be impossible for the cunningest Man on Earth to deceive the most innocent Creature living. But it seems high-time to break up, we'll continue this Subject some other time to a greater length; the Walks seem at present very entertaining, pray Ladies let's enjoy 'em.

With

With all my Heart, reply'd a Lady, but we ought first to choose, either the Countess or Sir W—— for entertaining the Company at our next Meeting.

The Countess was immediately pitch'd upon, who having given her consent, went with the rest to enjoy the innocent and pleasant Diversion of a Walk.

The Fifth ENTERTAINMENT.

NEver was Lover more punctual to an amorous Rendezvous, than this refin'd Assembly was careful to meet the next Day at the usual Place, where every one being seated, the Countess began the Discourse in the following manner.

For my part I must acknowledge myself altogether ignorant of the *Latin* Tongue, which was I perfect in, I should hardly confess it. Our Sex ought by no means to value it self on such Knowledge; and those Women who affect the Title of Learned, are seldom or never well fix'd in the World. Not that I approve the Ignorance most of us live in; I own we ought to use our utmost Endeavours towards the refining our Minds, by the Advantage we enjoy of reading. But let's take care how we flatter our selves in this Point; all Books are not in our Sphere; we ought to leave the more serious Studies entirely to the Men, and not profess our selves Mistresses of the *Greek* and *Latin*, but confine our Genius to the *Belles-Letters*, and be satisfy'd with what is sufficient to raise us a degree above the vulgar Ignorance. Authors of Gallantry suit us best; they refine our Wit, without puzling
our

our Senses; and we may find the Advantages of such Lectures, in our daily Conversation. Every one must allow *Ovid* of that Number; and 'tis with a vast Pleasure I always read his Works, translated into our Tongue. I find him every where expressing himself in a manner easy, tender, and agreeable; and the better to acquit myself of my Duty, I have endeavour'd as much as possible to come up to his Sense, in the following Precepts against Love. The first indeed seems to me very inconsiderable, but it mayn't however be improper to cite it.

(If you lie under an Obligation of frequenting those Places where your Mistress resorts, by a discreet Management of your Eyes and Countenance, conceal your Love. Seem designedly ungenteel, that your voluntary Negligence, which is an affront to her Beauty, may make her sensible you are no longer desirous to please her. Shun all particular Discourses, but if that's impossible, set a Watch upon your Mouth, that she may come off no gainer by your Indiscretion. Be insensible to her Tears, Oaths, and Protestations; which they most abound with, when they design nothing more than deceiving their unwary Lovers. Persuade your self, that her Heart is no faithfuller than the Tongue, which made no scruple of violating her Promises, and betraying your Vows. Your Resentments once animated by these Reflections, will give Reason the Soveraignty over your Heart; so that, how powerful soever your Inclinations be, her next Infidelity will keep the Balance even between her Beauty and your Love.)

I plainly see the Reason, Madam, says a Gentleman, why you can't approve of this Precept. Is it not that it argues a little to boldly with the Ladies,

Ladies, and speaks a Truth which even shocks 'em? You would have approv'd *Ovid* better, had he not advis'd such an Insensibility at your Tears and Protestations; though at the same time the Advice is absolutely necessary for us. We are often so credulous and instrumental to our own Deceit, that tho' a Lady has been guilty of the greatest Perfidy, we willingly persuade our selves that for the future she will certainly be more faithful; and we believe those Oaths we have so often seen violated. The only way is, continu'd he, utterly to defy your enchanting Promise, and take it for a general Rule, that a Mistress who has once shown herself false at the Expence of Lover's Oaths, will never be backward at repeating her Crime.

You argue not amiss Sir, reply'd Sir *W⸺*, But take my Word Love is not to be govern'd by Reason. A Person not engag'd, may make such Reflections; and foresee the dangers he is likely to incur, by surrendring his Heart to a Mistress, whose fickleness is even become a Town-talk: But the Moment he's captivated, he forgets his prudent Reasonings, he his not so curious for what may happen, nor will he give himself leave to anticipate his Pains by Reflection. In Love we flatter our selves, that the Charmer we have fix'd upon will renounce her usual Fickleness, and suffer herself to be conquer'd by Perseverance; that she'll be entirely ours, and in a Word, that we shall find no reason to complain of our Choice. We thus anticipate her Justification, and judging of her Heart by the Sincerity of our own, believe her Oaths inviolable, because she says, and we wish it so. How careful are we to avoid a forecast, that advises the quitting a Mistress, rather than running the

risque

rifque of her Falfhood? A Man muft love very coldly, that can form Defigns of this Nature; and it is impoffible a Flame fhould be of any ftrength, which the Apprehenfions only of a Miftrefs's Infidelity, are capable of extinguifhing.

I am of this Opinion, reply'd a Lady, and I alledge, a Fear of that Nature to be fo far from weakning a Paffion, that it rather adds Vigour to it. An eager Lover, under Apprehenfions of his Miftrefs's efcaping his Lures, redoubles his fervent Sollicitations, and thinks it poffible to raife a Love in her anfwerable to that, he has continually manifefted. He fancies he fhall overcome the Afcendant of the Stars, which Influence her to Inconftancy, and accordingly is more careful of a Bleffing, which he is in continual fear of lofing.

What you fay Madam, reply'd the Countefs, is true in one Senfe, but falfe in another. If the Lover you make mention of is fo defperately in Love, that whatever his Miftrefs be guilty of, can never make him entertain the leaft Thought of leaving her; then the fear of her Inconftancy will certainly augment his Paffion, and make him exert all his Force of Rhetorick to oblige the unfaithful one to a ftrict Obfervance of her Vows. But on the other hand, fhould this Lover be already fatigu'd with her feigning a Love, and ftrive to rid himfelf of an importunate and impertinent Miftrefs; thefe Reflections will be of great Service to him; and in my Opinion anfwer the Intent of 'em. But, continu'd fhe, tho' this Precept feem not fo advantageous; I durft fay, the following ones will be preferable, and more agreeable to your Humours.

(Never

(Never employ your self in reading the paſſionate Letters ſhe has ſent you, left by affecting your Heart they reingage it; ſacrifice 'em all to the Flames, and let your Love periſh with 'em. Fly too the Places which have formerly been Witneſſes of your amorous Diſcourſes, while ſhe was yet Faithful: Baniſh even her Picture; 'twill entertain a fatal Remembrance of her Charms, and eaſily reſtore Vigour to a dying Flame: While you love the Copy, 'tis morally impoſſible the Original ſhould be indifferent to you.)

In my Mind, ſays a Gentleman, this Counſel is very uſeful. A Lover may endeavour, but he'll never be able to extinguiſh his Flame, while he retains the very Things which are alone capable of fomenting it. They are ſo many Tokens of the Fair One's Love; they make him look back with Pain on his paſt Happineſs; they prove agreeable ſeducers of his Heart, and inſpire him with a deſire to renew a Paſſion, the Pleaſures of which are contiually repreſenting themſelves to his Idea. The ſight of a well-touch'd Picture, the Lecture of a paſſionate Letter are ſo many freſh Darts Love makes uſe of to wound the Heart. Such Objects awaken a drowſy Paſſion, and ſoon make him renounce the Deſign he had once taken up of no longer loving. He muſt baniſh all ſuch Amuſements, from a Love ill extinguiſh'd, and guard well his Eyes from any thing that may affect his Heart: Let him remember he can never be too cautious againſt Love.

Certainly, added the Divine, we can never be too much on our Guard againſt an Enemy whoſe offenſive War pleaſes us, and who makes uſe of us againſt our ſelves. We ſhould continually be in a Poſture of Defence againſt his Fury, and

F   ſhow

show our selves as brisk in defending our Hearts, as he is cunningly Vigorous in assaulting 'em. We ought especially, as *Ovid* says, to shun those Places that have so often heard our mutual plighted Oaths of eternal Fidelity; the sight of 'em is dangerous, and encourages such tender Reflections, as we ought by no means to engage our Thoughts in, if we really desire no longer to Love. See how beautiful the Expressions of *Berenice* to *Titus* are, in a *French* Tragedy of that Name; they speak the Author perfectly acquainted with the Passions of Mankind; and run to this Effect.

There's nothing I behold but wounds me fresh.
Where'er I turn my Eyes, where'er I move,
Every thing witnesses our mutual Love:
The myslick Cyphers of our Names appear,
And to my melancholy Passion are,
Such grand Impostures, as I cannot bear.

These Verses are really worthy the Poet, and the Queen that speaks 'em, reply'd a Lady; I'll add some others not less pathetick, though the Thought has not so much of the Sublime; and I don't question but you'll excuse the citing 'em when you hear how agreeable the Application is to the Subject in Hand.

Quick from the dangerous Place depart,
  There shady Greens,
  There murmuring Streams,
There Tircis first seduc'd my Heart.
I'll turn my Flocks and come no more,
Where the Ingrate so often swore.
My rebel Heart will not obey!
  In vain I strive,
  To part and live!
The perjur'd He,

Attracts me hither; my Feet cheat my Will,
And tho' I feign would go, I am here still.

These Lines lose nothing of their Beauty, by not having the modern Air of Novelty, reply'd Sir *W——*, the Shepherdess's Thoughts are express'd with a great deal of Life, and Nature speaks in every Word. The Amorous Conflict is describ'd without Art, and her innocent Expressions have some peculiar Charms, which must unavoidably be perceiv'd. Methinks I see this enamour'd Shepherdess, arm'd with her Crook, and endeavouring to divert her Flocks from the fatal Wood, where an unfaithful Lover had so often engag'd her; but she does it after a manner as plainly shews she would not willingly be obey'd; and at the least wandring on their part, seems rather enclin'd to follow 'em. She would quit the Place, but she has no Power; Love naturally attracts her thither against her will.

But it would be more advisable for her to resist that fatal Impulse, answer'd the Countess, her Misfortune would seem less aggravating; and I think some charitable Shepherdess should advise her to another Pasture. She would soon perceive the Benefit of this Remedy, in as great a degree as the generality of Lovers, will that of the following one.

('Tis not enough; you must yet go farther, and commit a Violence upon your Inclinations by not frequenting the *Theatre*. Good Comedies are dangerous to a Heart ill cur'd. A *Santlow* has such an absolute command over us, that she even inspires the Passion she imitates. Nor is the *Opera* less to be avoided; Dances well perform'd, Airs agreeably sung by a soft melodious Voice, join'd in Confort with Masterly Touches on Instruments; infpire the Soul with resistless Softness; and prove so many Arrows, that fatally pierce the yielding Heart. In a Word, harmonious Voices are no less imperiously powerful in Love than piercing Eyes.)

I believe, says a young Lady, the *Comedians* of *Ovid*'s time, were not a little incens'd at his Advertisement; and certainly our Modern ones would not think themselves less injur'd should we renew it now; not that I imagine it practicable. What? Live without *Comedies* and *Opera's!* I had rather be for ever depriv'd of the Pleasures you pretend to taste in Love, than to quit those real ones I find in *Comedies*, and especially in *Opera's*.

You must needs place an entire Satisfaction in such Diversions, Madam, reply'd a Gentleman, since you dare prefer 'em even to those we feel in loving. But I easily excuse your Opinion, since it proceeds from a Heart as yet insensible; but a thousand to one you change your Opinion e'er long: You'll grow nicer in the Choice of your Pleasures, and make a great difference between the Transports of the Heart, and the Amusements of the Mind: Not that I think *Opera's* so extremely dangerous to Lovers. Such Sights have nothing in 'em strenuous enough to produce the Effects we are apprehensive of; they rather surprize than affect us, and have greater Power over the Eyes than the Mind. They are not capable of exciting those Tendernesses, Love must owe its rise too; they raise not the Passions, and the Pomp that attends 'em never reaches the Heart; or if it does, 'tis so superficially, that the Impression is imperceptible. We go from an *Opera* full of Admiration, rather than Softness;

ness, and the Vanity that accompanies it, will not give us leave even long to admire; thus seeing our selves not at all affected with any part, we remember it no longer than we are present.

But 'tis a different Case with Comedy, which affects us in the most sensible manner, and touches us to the very bottom of our Hearts; softening, animating, and filling us with powerful Ideas. Lofty Expressions utter'd by a *Powell*, or any excellent Actor, makes a strange agreeable Confusion in the Mind; affects it every way, and leaves behind a deep Idea of the Part, he has so admirably personated. This ought however to be no reason for depriving our selves of the Entertainments of the Stage, which ought not to be held so offensive to the Amorous Heart: For tho' Love is the great Machine, nay the very Soul that actuates the *Theatre*; yet would we but examine Matters more curiously, we should find our selves less mov'd by the Hero's Love, that the Accidents and dangerous Consequences that usually attend it. The Author of *Sophonisba* gives a good Example of this: King *Massinissa* is in Love with *Sophonisba* even to Desparation; I must confess the manner of expressing his Passion is most affecting, but the Fate that attends it even amazing; it fills the Audience with Compassion, and he is universally pity'd, less as a Lover, than as being unfortunate, and at the last fatal. The furious Jealousy of *Mithridates*, produces the same Effects in favour of *Ziphares*; but the Audience rather laments the Perils he exposes himself to for *Monima,* than his violent Passion for her.

Add to this, reply'd the Divine, that a Tragedy where Love has the greatest share, may in some measure assist Lovers in overcoming their own Paffion. The attending Misfortunes which they are Eye-witneffes of, may undeceive 'em, make 'em apprehenfive of the like Dangers, and infpire 'em with an eager defire of avoiding a Precipice, where fo many have found their Fate: Love is feldom crown'd on the Stage; its Cataftrophe is always fad, and the moft paffionate Lovers are generally the moft unhappy. *Pyrrhus* finds his Fate at the Altar, where the Nuptials of *Andromache* were intended. *Alexander* reaps not the Fruit of his Perfidy to *Statira*, in quitting her Charms for thofe of *Roxana*, it ends in all their Deaths. Such Examples are not a little inftructive to Lovers; and in my humble Opinion, 'tis a wrong Method of proceeding, when we reprefent that for an infectious Poifon, which will prove in effect a wholefome Remedy.

You reafon very ingenioufly Sir, anfwer'd a Lady, but fay what you will, you'll fcarce perfuade me of the *Theatres* not encouraging Love; thoufands will tell you the contrary. But left I fhould engage my felf in a Queftion beyond my Sphere; I'll only hint, that in my Opinion 'tis indifferent, and only to be juftify'd by the various Ufe we make of it. It works divers Effects according to the diverfity of Hearts it meets with. An *Inamorato* will certainly encreafe his Flame; when another whofe only aim is to ftifle it, fhall by thefe means, fortify his Refolutions, and grow wife at others Expence. But generally fpeaking, Comedy is rather more apt to create than banifh Love, and I would never advife a Lover to feek a Remedy for his Paffion either at *Drury-Lane*, or the *Hay-Market*; and I believe the Countefs can give us a Remedy more *a-propos* from *Ovid*'s Spring.

Ovid

Ovid really has more, anſwer'd the Counteſs, but give me leave to reſign my place. It is very reaſonable that Sir *W———* ſhould take ſome trouble upon him in interpreting *Ovid*; and, leſt you might ſay I had encroach'd another's Priviledges; I have left him his Share, tho' indeed it is the leaſt Share of all, which is an Advantage we enjoy'd, by our entering the laſt on this Subject: I believe Sir *W———* no leſs ſatisfy'd with his Chance, than I with mine.

At theſe Words the Aſſembly roſe, to follow their ſeveral Inclinations; for my part I know nothing of the Matter, nor do I believe the Reader very ſollicitous to be better inform'd than I am.

The *Sixth* ENTERTAINMENT.

THE moment the Clock ſtruck Four, our Aſſembly met at the uſual Place; but was not a little ſurpris'd to miſs of Sir *W———* whom no one had ſeen ſince Dinner. They could not imagine the reaſon of his ſtaying ſo long, each was giving his Opinion, but none hit right. They had at laſt order'd a Footman to go ſeek him, when they perceiv'd him advancing towards 'em in great haſte. Ah! Gentlemen and Ladies, ſays he, I aſſure you 'tis no ſmall Difficulty to grope out an Author's Meaning: And having heard that purling Streams and Fountains were the Muſes delight, I took a ſober Walk immediately after Dinner, to reflect on the three following Precepts of *Ovid*. *Apollo* pardons you, Madam, continu'd he, addreſſing himſelf to the Counteſs, but you was in the wrong Yeſterday, in not concluding this Subject,

ject, when your Career was so hardly stop'd. You ought out of Charity to have included the following one however; I assure you it would have agreed incomparably well with those you have already handled.

(Avoid reading Romances, or Books of Gallantry, where Love-Intrigues fill every Page. Lovers are too easily flatter'd by 'em, and they always leave behind a Tincture of the Love which inspires 'em. Poetry is yet more advantageous to Love; it expresses a Passion so tenderly, that it is impossible not to be captivated; it fires the coldest Heart, and the moment you begin to read, you begin to love.)

I own it Sir, says a Gentleman, Poesy has mighty and prevailing Charms; 'tis a sweet Poison, an agreeable Enchantment, expresses Love to the Life, nor is any thing more proper to inspire a Passion than soft Verses. They cause an Emotion in the Soul not to be express'd, and 'tis with Pain we endeavour to overcome its pleasing Effects: The Heart suffers it self to be master'd, and lies open to all the Transports they inspire. But 'tis not every Poet can do this; very few can reach the Heart, and be guilty of this sweet Violence, which ought to be the only Aim of their Art; and which affects and transports the Reader beyond himself. Poesy is now almost monopoliz'd by the Stage, there it shews its greatest Efficacy, by ravishing the severest Audience; and is scarce known in other Places. The empty bundles of jumbled Words so long reigning in almost all our Modern Languages, are so faint and inexpressive, that it proves the greatest fatigue, but to read 'em; they are so void of the natural softness of a true Poet, that tho' they were assisted by the most willing Lo-

vers

vers Fancy, yet they would fall short of expressing a Passion with Energy. We have no melting Elegies, such as could triumph over the most insensible Lady's Cruelty, such as *Tibullus*, *Propertius*, and above all our *Ovid*, left the World excellent Models of. A Man blest with such Talents, might conquer universally; no one would be cruel to him, nor would he ever languish long without enjoying the Fruits of his Expectations.

I knew a very pretty Woman, answer'd a Lady, who never had the least thought of Poetry's prevailing Power; she would never receive a *Billet doux* from her Lover, but would make no scruple at the *Sonnets*, *Madrigals*, and *Epigrams*, which he was continually presenting her with. Pray how come that?

I'll tell you, reply'd another Lady, perhaps his Lover was so very indifferent a Poet, that she never apprehended his Verses powerful enough to make any Impression on her Heart.

There is yet another reason, reply'd Sir *W*——, perhaps this Lady was of the number of those, who have a thousand ridiculous Nicities in their imaginary Honour; and whose Virtue is more affrighted at the Name of Love, than as the Passion it self. A *Billet-doux* alarms the sham Modesty of these scrupulous Hearts; they think it an impardonable Crime to receive one, and at the same time are well-pleas'd with a Love-Elegy, which is in effect the same thing. For pray, what matters it, whether Love presents it self in Verse or in Prose? Is it less dangerous in a *Letter* than in a *Madrigal*? But because they imagine the first carries a much larger Signification, it is absolutely rejected, while the other is carefully perus'd under the sham Appearance of an Air

of

of Gallantry, the Consequences of which are altogether insignificant. Thus they skreen their Pleasure in hearing themselves ador'd, under this specious Pretext; are all the while improving Probabilities to their Advantage; and have the Secret of entertaining a Flame, spite of their conceited Womanish Reserve.

Sir W—— speaks with a great deal of Reason, reply'd the Divine, it is much better to act from the Heart; a Lady may acknowledge her Passion, provided it infringe not on her Duty: There is a certain allowable Softness and Compliance, which tends directly to one Period in all its designs. These eternal Prudes, proud of an imaginary unsociable Virtue, are often the least so in reality. We must live with more humaniz'd Ladies; and leave these Heroines to indulge themselves in their belov'd Romantick Sphere.

As to Romances, interrupted a Gentleman, if I am not mistaken, Sir W—— forbids Lovers reading 'em. I really can't comprehend his meaning, continu'd he, but in my Opinion, there is nothing more capable of disgusting a Lover than such Books: Can there be any thing more frivolous, or less reasonable than what they contain? What Man would not for ever renounce the Pleasures of loving, and of being belov'd, if he was to undergo all the honourable Fatigues a Hero in Romance is ever expos'd to? There's nothing but Misfortunes upon Misfortunes thro' their whole series of Action; and they have no sooner, after thousand Dangers past attain'd to the sight of their Mistresses, but some unforeseen Gyant, or enchanted Lady calls 'em away to more Glory. Far from forbidding Lovers the reading of such Trifles, I would advise it: Or

if

if I did forbid 'em, it would not be out of any apprehension of making 'em amorous, but for fear they might deprave the Imagination, and fill 'em with a thousand false Ideas, which may insensibly hurry 'em to Extravagance. I wonder to hear *Ovid* advise such Remedies.

Pray don't accuse *Ovid*, this Precept belongs not to him, reply'd the Divine, Sir *W——* gave it us voluntarily, the better to suit our Modern Follies. Such Books full of high, lofty *Expressions*, and void of Sense, were not known in *Ovid*'s Age; or if they were, they had not the absolute sway, they now bear thro' the vitiated taste of Mankind. But at length, thank Reason, we have disabus'd our Senses, and such fatiguing bombast Volumes have given place to more entertaining Novels, and Histories of Gallantry.—— Which are not at all preferable to Romances, interrupted a Gentleman, omitting some few, you find 'em so flat, and void of Entertainment, that they require much Leisure and more Patience to read 'em out. Never was Mankind more pester'd with ill Productions than in the present Age. Every one must write, 'tis a Disease every Wittling is infected with, and the itching Desire to see their Names in print, is so raging, that they are well contented to proclaim themselves ridiculous, if the World is but well satisfy'd of their being Authors. Here's one just come to Town; another that yet carries about him the Marks of Discipline; talks *Dutch, French* or *English,* but void of Learning, and unexperienc'd in Books well worded; yet this Fellow, nothing will serve him but writing a Book: Well; he begins by translating some unfortunate Author, (whose Sense he is so far from understanding, that he scarce is able to explain him

ver-

verbatim) into *English:* With this defign he felects fome doting Author, that has before doz'd over the fame Subject; and dictates his Periods after his Example, 'till having only chang'd fome of the Words, and thofe too for the worft; he tells the World he really underftands *English* no more than the Language he undertook to tranflate. Another refigning himfelf to his extravagant Fancy, and unbounded Imagination, fets himfelf to penning fome ridiculous Adventures, which he has the Confidence to call Novels. Now pray tell me, ought not this to be regulated? And in refpect to good Senfe, ought we not to have a Comptroller General of Wit, as well as a Juftice of Peace?

Stop your Career Sir, interrupted a Lady, your Enthufiafm has tranfported you a little too far; if the Books you feem fo inveterate againft, chance not to pleafe you, prithee don't read 'em, no one obliges you. All Men's Taftes are not fo delicately Nice as yours; many read for pleafure only, and are lefs follicitous for the Ufeful than the Agreeable. Hiftories of Gallantry are very proper to relax the Mind; and the very worft have fomething in 'em diverting. I think inftead of railing thus at our Modern Productions, you ought to give thofe Perfons Thanks, who wear themfelves out for our Entertainment: The very number of Authors is agreeable, and advantageous; it informs Foreigners, that Wit, and the Sciences reign among us, and that the prefent Age is no lefs eftimable for lively pieces of Wit than that of *Auguftus.* If fome new *Author* has the ill Fortune to difpleafe, be not however too hafty in condemning him; Time may produce, even from him, fomething more accomplifh'd. The firft Flight is never a Mafter-piece; Time

is

is requir'd for perfecting the Fruits of our Brain equally with those of the Earth: Never discourage a young Author by despising his first Works, nor make him in despair, utterly throw away his Pen; but on the contrary animate him by small Commendations, which may in the end prove so many Spurs to Perfection.

Here the Lady perceiving a Gentleman about making an Answer, address'd herself to Sir *W——* and said; I beg of you Sir to go on with your Design; I find this Gentleman has a Months mind to run out against our Modern Authors, to prevent him Sir, pray proceed with the following Precepts.

Sir *W——* oblig'd her by immediately taking up the Discourse, and saying,

(Would you entirely stifle your Flame, endeavour to deceive your self; and persuade your Heart, that the Object of its Affections is lovely in no others Opinion. I can't imagine whence this fatal Caprice comes, that we love most where there is greatest danger of an interposing Rival; this Apprehension rather doubles than lessens our Passion. He then that would cease loving, must no longer fear her Loss. If you're an Eye-witness of a Rival's daily Courtship, bear it patiently, shew no distaste, never appear Chagrin; look on both with Indifference, and if you have the Power to surmount your Anger and Jealousy, you'll soon dislodge your Love: But if you can contract a Friendship with your Rival, your Business is done.)

I'm of *Ovid*'s Opinion, answer'd the Countess, while a Man is Jealous he surely loves;

> *Should* Titus *Jealous prove,*
> Titus *does surely love.*

Jealousy

Jealousy is Love's Hand-maid, and certain Symptom, nor can any Person be plagu'd with the first, without an equal Share of the last. A Lover may flatter himself with his imaginary Liberty, but if he can't bear seeing his Mistress in his Rival's Arms, he still loves her. His Jealousy is the effect of a Passion, not so dead as he imagin'd; and lets him know he has vainly sung *Io Triumphe* before the *Victory*, assures him he did not examine his Heart thoroughly, when he entertain'd the fatal Opinion of having shook off his Chains; and in a Word that he still loves with the same Ardour, those Beauties, he is so jealous of losing: Since it is evident we are never sollicitous about the Loss of such Things as are wholly indifferent to us.

This Fear is not always caus'd by Love, reply'd a Gentleman, it is owing entirely to I know not what disgust a Lover retains in prejudice of those Beauties whose Coldness quashes his Passion. He is pleas'd, as a sort of Satisfaction, for the slight she made of him, to see her us'd in like manner by the rest of the World; he is enviously glad to find her Charms neglected; while she like a true Woman is Vaporous and Melancholy for being depriv'd of the Satisfaction of seeing a Crowd of Lovers sighing at her Feet: In a word he conceives a malignant Joy in beholding her, tho' undeservedly abandon'd by the gay part of Mankind. You see by this, continu'd he, that we are sometimes jealous without the Pain of loving, and are frequently fearful of seeing our Mistress in the Possession of a Rival, when our Flame is really extinguish'd.

You deceive your self Sir, reply'd a Lady, and the Lover you are describing is more deceiv'd than you: He must love in his Heart a Mistress

whom

whom he would willingly have no one else adore. You may term it Spite, Jealousy, or what you please; the Name's altogether indifferent; but I'm positive he feels the same Torture, the same Inquietude, as the most Jealous are tormented with. He may aim at hiding his Jealousy, and so endeavour to cheat himself, but his continual Vexation makes him sensible that he is the only Person ignorant of it. For after all, why should he be in such continual Pain for the loss of a Mistress, he pretends to have no Affection for? Ridiculous! No, no, let me tell you, he is still amorous, and all that can be said in his Favour, is, that he loves without knowing any thing of the Matter.

Without knowing any thing of the Matter, reply'd a Gentleman, is that possible?

Very possible, and very frequent, answer'd the Lady, and when you have heard the following Adventure, you'll make no longer doubt of it.

The History of FIDELIO and LYSANDER.

*F*Idelio had contracted a lasting Friendship with Lysander, who was likewise so firmly engag'd, that they never pass'd a Day without seeing one another. Lysander had a Sister, call'd Belinda, who put such an entire Confidence in her Brother, that her Love was wholly plac'd on him. She was Beautiful and Witty. Fidelio was well-shap'd and naturally gallant: They saw one another daily at Lysander's, who by his Father's Death became absolute at home: The Liberty he allow'd at his House, drew Persons of each Sex thither, to divert themselves in Matches of Gallantry and Pleasure. 'Twas in one of these set Matches that Lysander first entertain'd an Opinion, of Belinda's being sensible of Fidelio's Merit; he saw her Eyes con-

continually fix'd upon him; and was not displeas'd at the Birth of a Passion he had so long desir'd to foment. He immediately began to inspect his Friend's Conduct; but tho' he us'd his utmost endeavour, he could never so far sound his Mind as to be satisfy'd whither *Fidelio* really entertain'd those Thoughts in favour of *Belinda*, which he did not doubt her being sensible of in favour of him. *Fidelio* had a real Esteem for *Lysander*'s Sister, which he had not yet discover'd, 'twas with Eagerness he sought her; with Pleasure he saw her; he took his leave with torment of Mind, and look'd upon her as one of his best Friends: But as he never much examin'd his Heart on the Matter, he was a long time insensible of his Passion for her. *Lysander* all this time, tho' he made no doubt of *Fidelio*'s Power over his Sister's Heart, yet took no notice of it to him, who was too much his Friend to make a Mystery of his Love, had he been sensible of his Affection for *Belinda*. Six Months were pass'd in this huddle of Affairs. *Belinda* still loving *Fidelio*, us'd all her Artifice to conceal her Love from the Knowledge of the World, and especially her Lover; while *Fidelio*, not diving into the Cause of her Restraint, imagin'd she was either privately engag'd to some other, or (as he fancy'd himself) exempt from any settled Passion. At last *Polydore*, a young Person of Quality and vastly Rich, fell desperately in love with *Belinda*, by dancing with her at a Ball; and took an occasion the next Day to make *Lysander* a Visit, that he might have the Happiness of seeing his charming Mistress. It was impossible for him to see her this second time, and remain Master of himself; he immediately resolv'd to love her, and carry'd it so far on his side, that he was resolutely ly bent to demand her in Marriage. With this design he apply'd himself to *Fidelio*, whom every one perceiv'd to be a most intimate Friend of *Lysander*'s. Having made him a Visit, he open'd the Case, and beg'd the favour of him to use his utmost Interest with *Belinda*'s Brother for obtaining (the only honour he was ambitious of) an Alliance with his Family, by marrying his Sister. *Fidelio* was so surpriz'd at this Compliment that he scarce had the Power to make him an Answer; 'till *Polydore* a little nettled at his Neglect, ask'd him in a serious Tone, if he found any thing so very shocking in his demand, and whither he was not deceiv'd when he imagin'd he was addressing himself to a Friend. *Fidelio*, who by this time had recover'd himself, made the best excuse he could by laying the Blame on a Fit of the *Hippo*, and told him, tho' with great disorder, that he was ready to do him whatever Service he demanded; but that it would be convenient to apply himself to *Belinda*. *Polydore* assur'd him she would by no means oppose it, and that they only depended now on her Brother's Consent; that indeed he acknowledg'd it his Duty to demand his Mistress in Person, but that being satisfy'd of the strict Friendship they had contracted, he thought he could not address himself to a more proper Person, in a Case, on the Success of which his entire Happiness consisted. These last Words threw *Fidelio* into a disorder, he had never before been sensible of: He made a thousand Reflections on his Unhappiness, and accus'd himself as the only cause of his Confusion at so unaccountable an Adventure. He could no longer doubt his Love for *Belinda*; and not being able to comprehend by what Infatuation he was ignorant of it, sunk in a despair, the Vio-

G   lence

lence whereof, he could no longer master. He went to *Lysander*'s-irresolute whether he should see him: For his Desires were so confounded, that what with the fear of finding *Belinda* alone, and the Obligation he found himself under, of acquainting her with *Polydore*'s Design; he even blush'd at the Confusion he saw himself in. He found *Belinda* alone in her Chamber, leaning in a melancholy Posture on the Table; her Eyes fix'd on the Ground, with the Air of a Person full of trouble, and lost in a profound Thought. The Noise he made at coming in, disturb'd her, and rising somewhat hastily she shew'd some Concern for being surpriz'd in her *Meditations*; which he was the only insensible Cause of; for he employ'd her whole Mind. *Polydore*, who at leaving *Fidelio*, had made her a Visit, was that moment gone; 'twas he had put her into that visible Consternation, by the Assurance he had given her of *Fidelio*'s promoting his Passion, both with *Lysander* and herself. Madam, says *Fidelio*, addressing himself to her, am not I come inconveniently, thus to interrupt your agreeable Thoughts, and can you pardon my ill-timing the design I have to impart some Orders which have lately been enjoin'd me, tho' against my Will? I know what you would say, reply'd she, hastily, and will willingly spare you, if you think fit, the unnecessary trouble you must be at in recounting all *Polydore*'s Merit. I am sensible how much he deserves; I'll do him Justice, and as a Mark of it, I have this moment given him that Consent which you are so obliging as to demand in his favour. Her pronouncing these Words easily manifested the disorder and trouble of her Mind. *Fidelio* wholly ignorant how to apply her Words, was in the utmost Confusion for an Answer, when *Lysander* enter'd enter'd the Chamber. He took him aside; and having first inform'd him of a Quarrel, he was engag'd in with a *Gentleman*; and that he was expected at the appointed Place, desir'd his Assistance in form of a Second. *Fidelio*, who was rather enclin'd to Bravery than Love, tho' he found his very powerful in favour of *Belinda*; thank'd his Friend for the Opportunity he had given to shew how much he was his Friend, and without more Complements quitted the Room together, and went to the Field appointed for the Scene of Action. They only found the Person who had began the Quarrel, and were oblig'd to stay 'till his Second was come to engage *Fidelio*, who was unwilling to let 'em fight alone, while he remain'd an idle Spectator of the Combat. In a few Minutes, the other *Gentleman* came, and *Fidelio* immediately perceiv'd it to be *Polydore*, who without enquiring into the Quality of his Adversaries had engag'd himself for his Friend's Second, the moment he had parted from *Lysander's* House. Had he been inform'd, he would certainly never have agreed to this Proposal in a Juncture where *Love* and *Marriage* were in Agitation. We may easily guess his Surprize at seeing his chance Enemies, nor was *Fidelio's* less. But Honour allow'd no Reflections, the Business in hand was to be minded, and they were bent on nothing but Victory. *Lysander* after a long dispute with his brave Adversary, laid him dead at his Feet; while *Fidelio* having by many Wounds disabled, and at last disarm'd *Polydore*, oblig'd him for preservation of his Life, entirely to quit all thoughts of *Belinda*. The Combat thus finish'd, all Endeavours were us'd to hinder it spreading. The dead Body was privately dispos'd of; and *Polydore* retir'd into the Country 'till his Wounds were thoroughly cur'd. *Fidelio* confess'd to his Friend the Love he had for *Belinda*, and acknowledg'd himself at last convinc'd, that what he had so long mistook for the pure Effects of Esteem; seem'd at a nearer View, nothing more than a most ardent Passion. He declar'd himself to *Belinda*, and soon awaken'd in her Soul all the tender *Thoughts* she once had, but design'd no longer to entertain in his Favour; she now requites his Passion, with a willing charming Obedience, which her Brother encourag'd to compleat the Happiness of so deserving a Friend.

Well, continu'd the Lady, addressing herself to the *Company*, are you not satisfy'd by *Fidelio*'s Example, that it is posible to love, and yet be ignorant of it?

I was always of that Opinion, answer'd the Countess, what I wonder at is to see two *Rivals*, successive Lovers of the same Mistress, at the end prove intimate Friends. In my Opinion when one has once entertain'd a generous Flame, it is not easy so effectually to eradicate it, but there will yet remain some Sparks that will render it impossible for us to look upon the Person we have once ador'd with any but a Lover's Eye. These remains of Love inspire us with a secret Anger against the Man whose Endeavours tend to the usurping a Place in our fair one's Heart. We look upon his Pretentions as *Encroachments* on our *Priviledges*; we fancy him guilty of a sort of Robbery, and tho' we carry it never so fair outwardly, it is with difficulty we strive to persuade our selves not to hate him. So that, continu'd he, I am not of *Ovid*'s Opinion, where he says, a Lover may carry his Indifference for a forsaken *Mistress*, even to contracting a Friendship with his *Rival*; and if you'll allow me Proof from this Lady's

Ad-

Adventure; let me tell you it is not in the least probable that *Polydore* ever had any Friendship with *Fidelio*, tho' he owes his Life to his *Generosity*.

I agree with you, Madam, reply'd a Gentleman, it is really a great rarity to see two Rivals carry it fair to one another, much less enter into a strict Alliance. Lovers no more than Kings can admit any Competitors, and the mutual Caresses of Rivals, are frequently with Reason suspected, and are often found dangerous at the Bottom.

I can embrace the Rival I'd destroy,

says a Tyrant. But there are to be found such Rivals as can agree admirably well together. No Disputes, no Contests, they visit their Charmer alternately, and the first comer honourably gives place at the other's arrival; or else they entertain themselves mutually, and mutually share the Fair one's Favours.

Impossible, replies another Lady, you'll never make me believe we have such patient Fools in the World, as to suffer such a Partition, without murmuring. He must certainly never love that can be so stupidly easy, as not to be mov'd at his Rival's Happiness. Love is more impetuous; He admits no Lukewarmness in his Dominions; he forces our Inclinations; pushes home; fires the cold, and fixes the roving Heart.

I'm of your mind, Madam, reply'd Sir *W——*, but I dare swear you'll disagree with me in the following Precept.

(There is but one Remedy remains, which leaves, if nothing else proves advantageous, the entire Cure to *Bacchus*'s Care. The Charms of the Bottle, with an innocent agreeable Debauch, must then banish the Torments of Love from a languishing Heart. A Boon-Companion seldom
loves

loves much; and the Bottle affords him more Charms than the most accomplish'd Beauty breathing. A Monarch's Satisfaction is not comparable to that he feels, when free from Cares, he quaffs his moderate Glass. Nothing can then interrupt his Happiness, he drowns Melancholy and Love, in a Bumper, and generous Wine has with him, the Effects of the River of *Lethe*, those Waters of Oblivion in the *Elysian Fields*.)

Certainly I shall never comply with you in this Point, says the Lady, nor can I believe you will have many Followers. I would not for *Ovid*'s Honour have heard a Precept, which may indeed suit a *Swiss* or *German*, but will hardly ever agree with the Gentlemen of our Island. Our Nation is too reasonable, and too refin'd; (without considering the Enmity it has to any thing that may shock Gentility) to have recourse to a Remedy, which in my Opinion is worse than the Evil it pretends to cure.

I see no reason, Madam, answer'd a Gentleman for your blaming this Advice, and accusing it as infringing the Rules of good Breeding. Is it not allowable to divert our selves with a select Company of Friends? Our Laws no ways forbid a moderate Glass, especially when its Advantages are so obvious? Love is the greatest and most dangerous of all Diseases, since it resides only in the Heart; we ought to use all our endeavours to dislodge it; and the Remedy *Ovid* now offers is by no means to be rejected. The Pleasure of drinking in a chosen Company, is only capable to dissipate, or at least to ease a Lover's *Torments*; the general Liberty that reigns there, the Joyialness, which is its inseparable *Concomitant,* can make him forget the Rigours of a Mistress; and prove himself careless and indifferent as she pretends to be. Pray

Pray hold Sir, interrupted a Lady, and don't shew your self a good *Advocate* in a bad Cause. I don't think a Gallant *Inamorato* would owe his Cure to such a Remedy; and tho' you argue so strenuously in its Favour, I must do you the Justice to say, that I am almost positive you would never have recourse to this Remedy, was the Case yours. But come Sir, continu'd she, addressing herself to Sir W——; pray proceed, that the next *Precept* may take away the fulsome Ideas of this.

I have already told you, Madam, answer'd Sir W——, that I had concluded. *Ovid*'s *Precepts* go no farther; the Work is now accomplish'd, and I had the Honour of giving it the finishing Stroke.

The Work accomplish'd, cry'd the Lady, prais'd be great *Apollo*, we are here become *Authors*; I really thought for my part I should never have enter'd myself in their Society, but I see we ought never to despair.

However we must keep this from taking Air, reply'd another Lady, our very intimate Friends will esteem us less, should they by any means come to know, that we have made a Book. I think we must give Mr.—— the trouble of compiling these *Six Discourses* in a Body; and publish 'em under the Title of *Remedies for Love*; by this means our *trouble* will turn to some *Account* with *Lovers*, for whose sake it was undertaken. The whole *Assembly* consented to her Proposal, and she immediately pursu'd.

Since our *Book* is finish'd, pray let us in the first place bid utter Defiance to the ordinary Prepossession of Authors in favour of their own Works; and with a real Sincerity, give our Opinions on this. Do you believe, continu'd she addressing herself to the *Company*, that our Remedy will infallibly cure a Love-sick Heart?

No Madam, reply'd a Gentleman, I can entertain no such thought. I am of the same Opinion with a Person of Quality, who says in one of his Moral Reflections. *There are variety of Remedies for Love, but none infallible.* *Ovid* is of the same Mind, and says, He will not endeavour to extinguish the *Urchin*'s *Torch*, clip his *Wings*, or steal away his *Quiver* and *Bow*, but that his only design is to advise in the Case. And I say after his Example, that these Advices are too often useless. A Man really in Love can by no means make use of 'em; Love fortifies his Heart against the wholesomest Counsel, and make him more

en-

enclinable to hear some *Method* for accomplishing his design; than the most moral Reason you can offer to the contrary.

I agree in this Sir, reply'd Sir *W——*, but at the same time must confess, that there are certain *Crititcal Minutes* when a Lover may make a true use of these Remedies. The Rage he is in at seeing a *Rival* prefer'd, while he is neglected; the small hopes he can reasonably entertain of his fair One's being more favourable to him; all this concurring may bring him to himself, and make him take a generous Resolution to quit his Chains. Thus he may gain by our *Remedies*, and make use of 'em with the same Joy a Ship-wrack'd Person would grasp a floating Plank.

I approve what Sir *W——* says, added the *Divine*, there are *Remedies* for the *Diseases* of the *Mind*, equally with those of the Body; and would a Lover but assist his own reason with our Counsel, I fancy he would find himself perfectly recover'd,

But Gentlemen and Ladies, since every one must give their Verdict, interrupted a Lady, it seems to me, as tho' all *Ovid*'s *Precepts* were more immediately calculated for the Gentlemen, and that the Ladies have small Interest in 'em. Pray how comes that? Does *Ovid* imagine we have no occasion for 'em.

They may indifferently serve for both Sexes, reply'd Sir *W——*, and you have the liberty of selecting those, you think most convenient and agreeable. Not that I hold 'em very necessary for you; the Ladies rarely love, without being belov'd, and these *Precepts* tend only to those, whose hard fate it is, not to have their *Passion* repaid.

The Lady was just returning Sir *W——*'s *Civility*, when they perceiv'd a *Footman* making towards 'em in great haste: He was come from *London* to inform her of her *Husband*'s Arrival from the *Army*; and that he impatiently expected her *Company*. Such agreeable *News* rejoic'd the whole *Assembly*, who unanimously persuaded her to go, that she might have the *Happiness* of his *Company*, whose entire Satisfaction depended on her.

Thus broke up this *agreeable Assembly*, having finish'd their *Sixth* and last *Discourse*; which must unavoidably give an *inexpressible Satisfaction* to the *Gallant Reader*.

FINIS.